Sir Seth Thistlethwaite

and the Soothsayer's Shoes

Written by Richard Thake
Illustrated by Vince Chui

King Philip Fluster IV
Queen Beth Fluster
Lady Sheri-Sue
Sir Shawn Shrood
Middle Thatchwych
Kingdom of Thatchwych
Lower Thatchwych
Southernmost Thatchwych
A
South Aybee Sea

Map Legend
A - Thatchwych Castle
B - Poxley Castle
C - Village of Euphoria
The road to Euphoria
The tunnel
The Prince's shortcut
Fire-breathing Bog Bats
Prince Quincy of Poxley
Kingdom of High Dudgeon
Edith-Anne
The Evil Weevil Woods
King Wally
Bog Runners
Swish, Swoosh, and Bruce

Owlkids Books Inc.
10 Lower Spadina Avenue, Suite 400, Toronto, Ontario M5V 2Z2
www.owlkids.com

Distributed in Canada by Raincoast Books
9050 Shaughnessy Street, Vancouver, British Columbia V6P 6E5

Distributed in the United States by Publishers Group West
1700 Fourth Street, Berkeley, California 94710

To Cameron and Duncan,
who constantly remind me how much fun it is to be a kid.

Library and Archives Canada Cataloguing in Publication

Thake, Richard, 1938-
Sir Seth Thistlethwaite and the soothsayer's shoes / Richard Thake, Vince Chui.

ISBN 978-1-897349-92-2 (bound).--ISBN 978-1-897349-93-9 (pbk.)

I. Chui, Vince, 1975- II. Title.

PS8639.H36S57 2010 jC813'.6 C2010-900548-1

Library of Congress Control Number: 2010920604

Design: Barb Kelly

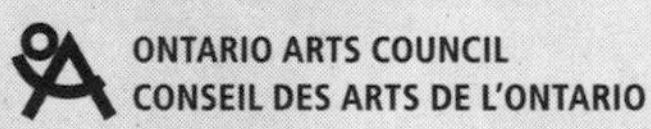

We acknowledge the financial support of the Canada Council for the Arts, the Ontario Arts Council, the Government of Canada through the Canada Book Fund (CBF), and the Government of Ontario through the Ontario Media Development Corporation's Book Initiative for our publishing activities.

Manufactured by Friesens Corporation
Manufactured in Altona, MB, Canada in March 2010
Job # 54073

A B C D E F

CONTENTS

6:0

1 Meet the MIGHTY KNIGHTS

Seth Thistlethwaite didn't know how he knew that he knew it, but something, somewhere inside his still-sleeping mind, started whispering: *Seth, it's morning again…*

He cautiously opened one eye, and out in the dew-dappled distance, the yellowish fringe of first light slowly tiptoed into the night. It crept past the still-twinkling stars, announcing that another knightly new day was getting ready to get under way.

Seth threw back the sheet, and as his feet touched the floor, he was suddenly Seth Thistlethwaite no more.

In his stead, from his bed, stood none other than Sir Seth Thistlethwaite the fearless and famous ten-year-old knight! And in the exciting world of his wild and wonderful imagination, he was about to set out—as knights did in those days—to seek out injustice and uphold fair play and rescue fair maidens from fire-breathing dragons and, if time allowed, slay all those miserable, invisible things hiding under your bed.

But his main job as a knight was to take all that was wrong in the world and make it suddenly right.

Before Sir Seth could go galloping gallantly forth, however, he realized he had forgotten to saddle his horse. For there, still asleep by the side of his bed, lay his faithful steed, Shasta—

who, in the half light between morning and night, looked more like a snoring golden retriever than she did a horse.

"Hey, Shasta," Sir Seth whispered softly into one ear. "Come on, girl. It's Saturday. Time to get up and get going. We've got a lot of knightly things to do today."

And so it was, on that memorable morning—after brushing his teeth and donning his armor—that Sir Seth Thistlethwaite stood at his front door and surveyed the wondrous new day. He hoisted the beat-up old broomstick that served him as both broadsword and lance and secretly signaled to his very best friend and next-door neighbor, Ollie Everghettz, that another day filled with mighty deeds was afoot.

Before you could say "toy boat" ten times fast, Sir Ollie arrived at the edge of the hedge also attired in magnificent knightly—but somewhat unsightly—tinfoil armor held in place by shoelaces and duct tape and Scotch tape and wire.

"By golly, Sir Ollie, you look ready to ride," Sir Seth said as he slipped Ollie the secret handshake of the Mighty Knights of Right & Honor—a handshake so deeply secret, I can't tell you more about it right here. Because there are spies of all sizes—in all kinds of disguises—lurking and working all over the place. And they all could be reading this page right now, the same as you!

"Yep. Saddled and ready, Sir Seth," Sir Ollie replied.

Together, the two knights errant started off another imaginary adventure in search of deeds that needed doing.

"Where are we going today?" Sir Ollie asked.

Sir Seth unrolled a scroll from inside his shirt. “Um... the king of Thatchwych needs our help.”

“Thatchwych? Where’s that?”

“It doesn’t say,” Sir Seth sighed. “But the king wants to see us in his castle right away. Ahhhh! Perhaps this fair maiden can tell us the way.”

Sir Ollie followed Sir Seth’s pointing hand and...lo and heigh-ho and hey nonny-oh, there below in a field filled with freshly flattened phlox lay a fair maiden, most forlorn and afraid.

“My lady,” Sir Seth said with a chivalrous bow, “we have been summoned to Thatchwych Castle by King Philip Fluster the Fourth. Could you tell us the way?”

“We, uh, can’t tell you any more than that, if you know what I mean,” Sir Ollie tried to advise her, with a wink and a bow of his own.

"Thatchwych, you say?" She smiled sweetly. "And by what name would I know you, sir knight?"

"I am Sir Seth Thistlethwaite at your service, my lady." He bowed again briefly with a sweep of one arm. "And from what awful thing might we save you this day?"

"Did you just say you're...Sir Seth Thistlethwaite?" she shrieked shrilly in open-mouthed awe, not far from faint. "Pray tell, sir, are you the selfsame Sir Seth Thistlethwaite of Mighty Knights legend and fame?"

"Yes, my lady, I am one and the same."

"You are? Ohhhhh, that's just too, too gigantically, frantically cool to be true!" she gasped in stunned disbelief. "You are none other than the seventh brave brother of Sirs Keith and Heath Thistlethwaite, and Brad, Chad and Thad, as well as the wondrous and thunderous Sir Thor Thistlethwaite, too?"

"Yes, my lady, I assure you that's who I am," Sir Seth muttered with all the modesty he could muster. "How may I be of service to you?"

"Oh, good sir knight, our prayers have been answered." She swooned and fell back with a thud. "I have been sent by King Fluster to greet you and meet you this day. So not only might you be of service to me—I can also be of service to you."

"I bid you, my lady, please explain."

She drew a deep breath, so excited she could barely speak. "I have been sent to guide you through Thatchwych to the evil, awful kingdom of High Dudgeon—where

Prince Quincy of Poxley dwells."

Sir Seth was completely confused. "High Dudgeon?"

"Yeah, and, uh, who's this Prince Quincy of Poxley?" Sir Ollie asked rather nervously.

"Let me explain. My father, Sir Shawn Shrood, who is the wise soothsayer of the kingdom of Thatchwych, has had his magical soothsaying shoes tragically stolen away by some evil thief, sent no doubt by that wart-nosed Prince Quincy of Poxley! Or had you not noticed that nowhere on this sunshiny day is there a snippet of sooth to be found anywhere?

"That's why King Fluster summoned you—to go to High Dudgeon and bring back those shoes!"

Sir Seth gasped with sudden respect. "You are... Lady Sheri-Sue Shrood?"

"Yes." She blushed shyly.

"My lady," Sir Seth uttered in awe, "you can depend on Sir Ollie and me to help you, however we can."

The more Sir Seth pondered Lady Sheri-Sue's problem, though, the more he shivered with knee-knocking shock—from the tip of his nose to the tops of his falling-down socks—at the sinking, brow-wrinkling, unthinkable thought of a kingdom without any sooth.

But before pursuing Sheri-Sue's most pressing problem, Sir Seth had a rather embarrassing confession to make.

"Um...well, as strange as this sounds and to tell you the truth, I'm afraid I've never heard of the word 'sooth.'"

Sheri-Sue stared at Sir Seth, both dazed and amazed.

"You claim to be a Mighty Knight, yet you don't know the word 'sooth'? I thought every knight knew that it's quite simply the olden-day word for...the truth!"

Sir Seth looked at her in stunned surprise. "The truth?"

"Yes. The truth," she said surely. "And until my father's magical truth-saying, soothsaying shoes can be returned to their rightful left and right feet, there's no way of knowing who is telling the truth anymore."

Without any truth, the kingdom of Thatchwych certainly seemed to be in quite a frightful muddle. Trying to imagine a truthless and soothless Thatchwych was like trying to imagine a day without being licked by your dog.

"So the shoes have magic in them," Sir Ollie gasped.

"Yes—a very special magic!" Sheri-Sue said excitedly. "From the Truth Fairy herself. Her very words when she gave them to my father were:

No matter what it is ye seek,

With these shoes upon your feet,

The truth shall dwell in all ye speak."

Sir Seth turned to Sir Ollie. "There's only one thing to do, Lady Sheri-Sue. The Mighty Knights must foray forth and bring back those shoes!"

"Oh, sir knight, that's what I was so hoping you'd say," she sighed, with a tiny tear in one eye.

Sir Ollie tugged at Sir Seth's tinny sleeve. "Uh, this assignment sounds like it could be kinda tough."

"Tough?" Sir Seth smiled. "That shouldn't be a problem for you. I've heard that the tough ones are the only ones that Everghettz ever gets. Isn't that true?"

"Yeah...I suppose so," Sir Ollie had to agree.

The mere thought of this exciting new quest made Sir Seth feel sort of fuzzy and wuzzy inside. And tingly and light. He drew his battle-scarred sword and knelt on one knee. "Tell me, my lady, where is this evil, awful kingdom of High Dudgeon? We will be on our way this very day."

Lady Sheri-Sue sighed sadly. "It is the awfulest, most unlawfulest place in the whole world, thick with fog-shrouded forests and foot-sucking bogs, where the swamplands were created from billions of butterflies' tears...and the sun hasn't been seen for more than three thousand years. The whole place is infested with weevils and weezils and elephant ants with measles. It's so awful and evil, I fear, that even the King's Kung Fu Fusiliers won't go near it, I hear."

In that instant, Sir Seth knew he must go there and give it a try. So with a flourish, he raised his sword to the sky. "No matter how bad High Dudgeon might be, it couldn't be worse than Thatchwych would be without any sooth!"

"Uh...right," Sir Ollie sort of agreed. "But what about all those warty weevils and weezils and stuff?"

"Never fear," Sir Seth assured him. "We have our trusty swords, and if everything else fails, we still have those magical meatloaf sandwiches my mother just made."

The mere mention of meatloaf brightened Sir Ollie a bit. "Who knows? Maybe wallowing around in bogs

full of weevils and weezils could be more fun than I thought." He could tell Sir Seth was itching to leave. "And don't forget the oath of the Mighty Knights of Right & Honor—'A true knight will do whatever it takes to take a wrong and turn it into a right.'"

"Right!" Sir Seth agreed. "Now all we need to know is which way to go."

"I can guide you," Sheri-Sue offered. "But I dare not venture farther into High Dudgeon."

"Nor do you need to, my lady," Sir Seth said. "This quest is a test for the Mighty Knights of Right & Honor! Shall we go?"

And so, with Lady Sheri-Sue leading the way, the Mighty Knights and their mighty dog, Shasta, started across Thatchwych on their way to the creepy, crawly kingdom of High Dudgeon.

2
The MAGIC Shoes

Sir Seth and Sir Ollie and—from time to time—their steed, Shasta, followed Sheri-Sue through the very old, merry old, frightfully delightfully old cuckoo-clock kingdom of Thatchwych.

"Gee, Thatchwych sure is beautiful," Sir Ollie said as they crossed a meadow of knee-deep yellow marshmallow puffs soaking in the sun.

"It's pronounced *Thatch'itch*," laughed Sheri-Sue.

"Thatch'itch? Sounds like a sneeze." Sir Seth grinned.

"Is it always this quiet?" Sir Ollie asked, looking around.

"Oh, Thatchwych is very sleepy and sheepy. And Little Bo-Peepy. And it's usually quite quiet most of the time. Except for one day in the middle of May, when Upper Thatchwych slid all the way down the side of Thatch Mountain."

Sir Ollie stopped and stared at her. "The whole place slid down the mountain?"

"Into the sea?" Sir Seth gasped.

"Yes. It must have been quite exciting to see. It all began way up at the tippymost top of cloud-shrouded Thatch Mountain, where soggy old, foggy old Upper Thatchwych huddled unhappily in the unending snow.

Then, early one morning, without any warning, Upper Thatchwych couldn't stand to be stranded up there in thin air for one more damp day—so in a shivering, sniveling snit, it simply slid down the side of Thatch Mountain. And landed with a spectacular splash and a three-day-long sigh of relief in the yummy, summery waters of the South Aybee Sea. It even took Thatchwych Castle along for the ride."

"Then what happened?" Sir Seth gasped.

"Well, it created quite a problem, because it meant that Upper Thatchwych—which had always been at the top—was now under Lower Thatchwych. Which, in turn, meant that both of them were now below Middle Thatchwych. Which was now at the top and not in the middle.

"Well, you can imagine the confusion it created for King Philip Fluster the Fourth, who was the king of all three of the Thatchwyches. He no longer could tell which Thatchwych was which."

"So what did he do?" Sir Ollie asked, also trying to figure out just what Thatchwych was where.

"He turned to his wife, good Queen Beth Fluster, for one of her good queenly suggestions.

"'What do you think we should do, dear?' the king asked.

"The queen smiled sweetly. 'I think we should do, dear, what we always do, dear, when we have a perplexing problem we can't seem to solve—let's summon that wonderfully wise adviser and all-knowing soothsayer, Sir Shawn Shrood, and see what enlightening insight he can shed on the day.'"

“I’ll bet he used his shoes to save the day!” Sir Ollie said excitedly, slapping Sir Seth on the back.

Sheri-Sue nodded and popped a plump yellow marshmallow puff into her mouth.

“Indeed he did!” she said proudly. “My father is the wisest adviser in all of the land. He’s so frightfully insightful and incredibly smart, the owls and the elders—and often even the elves themselves—come to him whenever they don’t know what else to do.”

She handed Sir Ollie a marshmallow puff. “It’s even said that my father’s so incredibly smart, he knows thirteen things that haven’t been thought of by anyone yet!”

“What is it?” Sir Ollie wanted to know.

“A yellow marshmallow. Try it. It’s good.”

“How do his shoes make magic?” Sir Seth asked, picking a yellow marshmallow for himself.

“I don’t really know,” Sheri-Sue admitted. “The secret was put in there by the Truth Fairy—and only she knows.”

“So what about King Fluster?” Sir Seth urged her.

“Ah, yes. Well, he called to the guards to summon my father.

"'Summon Sir Shawn Shrood!' the king called. 'Bid him come to the castle as quickly as he can!' But my father was already standing there, right by his left side—where he stood every day!

"'Ah! Here so soon, are you?' the king cried in surprise, as he did every time he summoned Sir Shawn. 'Good, good! Thank you for hurrying so. I, um, have a bit of a problem I was hoping you might resolve.'

"'Certainly, Sire,' my father said. 'I'll be happy to help you however I can.'

"The king paused, trying to get the problem straight in his mind. 'Um...well, it seems that Upper Thatchwych, which—quite rightfully, all day and all nightfully—should be at the top of Thatch Mountain, is instead soaking its socks in the South Aybee Sea. Not only that...'

"But my father interrupted the king with the wave of one hand. 'The solution is quite simple, Sire,' he said.

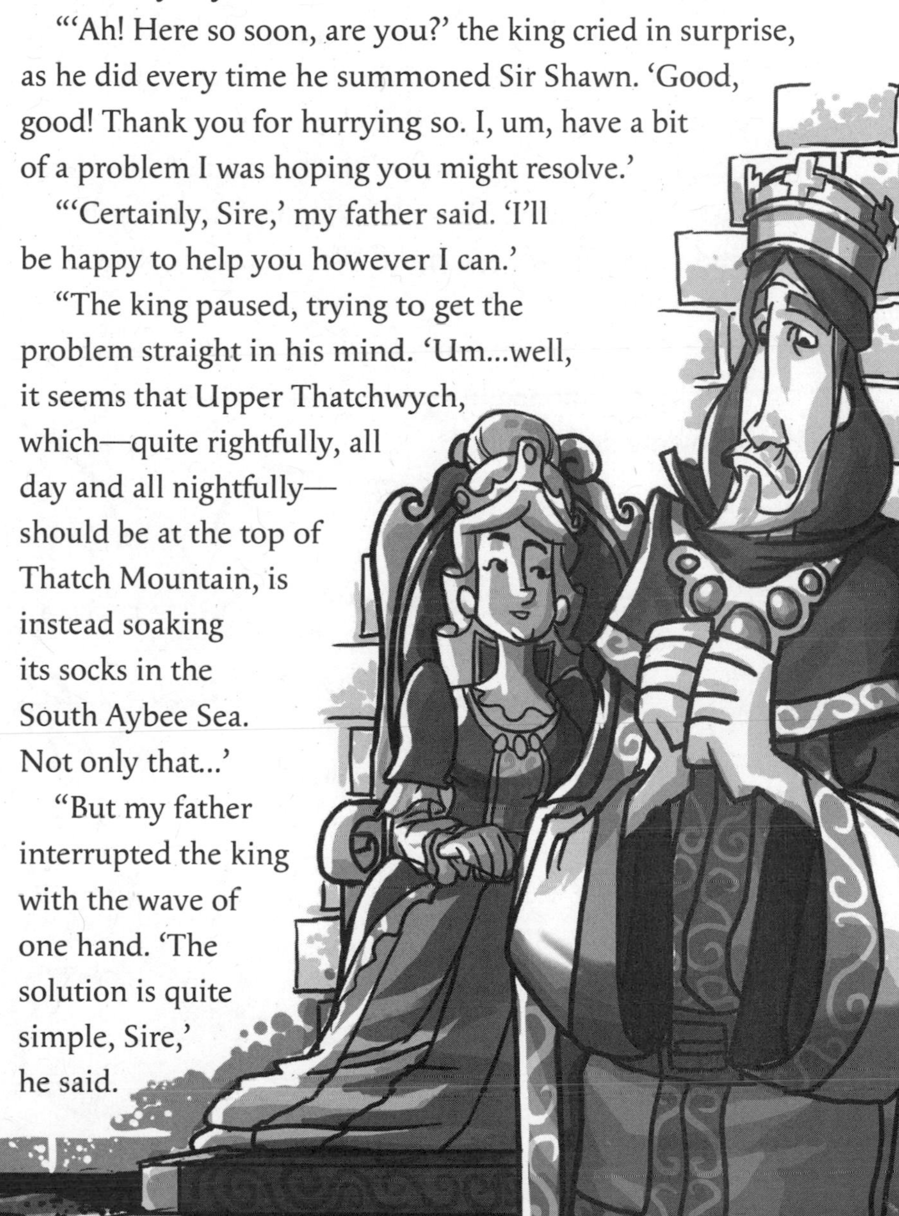

"'All that has changed is that Upper Thatchwych is now at the bottom of the mountain. Middle Thatchwych is still above Lower Thatchwych, which is where it always has been...'

"'Yes, yes,' the king replied. 'The middle is at the top.'

"'Well, Sire, might I suggest that you call the new county Southernmost Thatchwych? And let the others remain just as, and just where, they always have been?'

"'Southernmost Thatchwych,' the king uttered in awe, testing the two new words on his tongue. 'How utterly soothful and resoundingly right! Well done, Sir Shawn. So it shall be.'

"Then, to make everything legally and regally right, King Philip summoned his scribes and forthwith issued the following decree:

My dear, dear loyal subjects,

Because Upper Thatchwych, as you most clearly can see, is no longer above Middle Thatchwych, the new county shall heretofore and henceforth be known, by solemn and royal decree, as Southernmost Thatchwych! And to celebrate its most welcome and rousing arrival, it gives me great pleasure to declare free ice cream all year for everyone here. And no school for thirty-three days!

"Wow, free ice cream!" hooted Sir Seth.

"No school for thirty-three days!" shouted Sir Ollie.

"Actually," Sheri-Sue giggled, "it lasted for forty-three days—because nobody was keeping count. Everywhere, everyone was singing and bells were ringing and there was dancing and laughter throughout the land."

Just then, the three of them reached the top of a ridge—and for the first time, there was the dreaded, dreary kingdom of High Dudgeon.

Sheri-Sue shuddered. "Well, there it is, sir knights. Welcome to High Dudgeon."

"Wow. It sure is...dudgeony, isn't it?" said Sir Ollie.

"And somewhere in there is a pair of shoes we must find," Sir Seth whispered. "Where could they be?"

Sheri-Sue took their hands. "Please, all of Thatchwych is counting on you to bring back my father's shoes. He just sits in his tower, day after day, worried that he will give someone the wrong advice. Sir Seth, Sir Ollie, only you can bring the sooth back to Thatchwych."

Sir Seth suddenly straightened and took out his sword. "I promise you, my lady, a Mighty Knight goes wherever he must go and does whatever he must—"

Sir Ollie hoisted high his Mighty Knight banner. "To prove we are knights whose word you can trust!"

They knelt in front of Sheri-Sue and looked up into her face. "And when our word has been given, a promise is a promise...no matter what!"

"C'mon, Sir Ollie," Sir Seth cried. "Let's ride!"

3 Double-YUCKY High Dudgeon!

The prickly thickets of grumbling bumbleberry bushes were already awake and irate, as their plump clumps of busily buzzing yellow-and-black-striped berries grumpily greeted another dreary, uncheery High Dudgeony day.

"Hey, Sir Seth, what kind of bushes are these?" Sir Ollie asked as he poked one of the busily buzzing blossoms with El Gonzo, his sword. "They sure don't sound too friendly to me."

"Don't touch 'em, Sir Ollie!" Sir Seth tried to warn him. But he'd left it too late. The grumbling berries had already swooped down in a swarm and gnawed off the end of his sword.

"I see what you mean!" Sir Ollie exclaimed, jumping back three feet and falling in a heap on the ground. "How come they're so grumpy and jumpy like that?"

Sir Seth just smiled and helped Sir Ollie to his feet. "I guess High Dudgeon just makes 'em that way. You'd be grumpy and jumpy, too, if you lived here all day."

Walking in the footsteps of their faithful steed, Shasta, the two friends warily began wending their weary way. Past the still-grumbling bumbleberry bushes. Deep into the darkest swirling fogs of High Dudgeon. As they cautiously crept along the overgrown path, Sir Seth was instantly aware of the whispering silence that hung like a ghost in the nose-high grasses and rushes and weeds. Not a chirp of a cricket brightened the air. Not the scream of a blue jay could be heard anywhere. Everything, everywhere, was as ominously hushed as the bark of a tree.

All the plants and all the trees seemed snittish—rather upset at the incredible gall of three strangers being in High Dudgeon at all. They snapped at Sir Seth's ankles and grabbed Sir Ollie's clothes. One even nipped Shasta on the end of her nose.

Sir Seth was beginning to feel just a weeny bit worried about keeping the promise he had made to Lady Sheri-Sue. Then he felt in his pocket and there it was—the reassuring touch of the magical meatloaf sandwiches his mother had made. The moment he felt them, all the courage that had begun to wander away suddenly returned in a rush.

"Hey, Sir Seth," Sir Ollie whispered, suddenly wanting to know, "what does a weezil look like?"

Sir Seth thought about it briefly. "Well, y'know, I haven't actually seen a weezil. But I hear they're sort of round and dark brown and about the size of your fist, with a tail four feet long. They wind all around you, then hammer their heads on your knees until they knock themselves out. Why do you ask?"

"Oh, nothin'," Sir Ollie still whispered, without wondering why. "Well, then...uh, what does a weevil look like?"

Sir Seth had to think a bit longer than before, before he was able to come up with a guess. "Well, a weevil's a lot like a weezil, except, of course, it's about the size of a horse...and maybe even meaner and leaner and more awful than a weezil."

"Awfuler than a weezil? Yeah? Like how?"

"Um...well, they live up in trees and they're kind of stupid and slow. And if you walk under them, they'll drop on your head like a hat."

"So? What's so awful about that?"

"Well, like I said, they weigh as much as a horse," Sir Seth said with a shudder. "And if that's not bad enough, they cling to your lips so they can grab your food before you can eat it yourself. But the absolute worst thing about weevils is that they only eat cake and dessert."

"Oh, no!" Sir Ollie gasped at the thought. "They eat all your cake and dessert? What an awful way for a good knight to die."

Suddenly, Sir Seth had that creepy-crawly feeling that there was something bothering Sir Ollie. "Okay, Sir Ollie, what's up? How come you're asking me about weevils and weezils and stuff?"

"Well, uh, see that knobbly tree up ahead? The one that sorta looks like a witch?" Sir Ollie pointed out. "I think I just saw it twitch."

"Twitch?"

"Yeah. Up at the top. Do you think there might be a weevil up there gettin' ready to drop?"

Sir Seth stared into the silently swishing swirls of mist up ahead, trying to see if the tree was really twitching—or whether it was Sir Ollie who was twitching instead.

Then, just as Sir Ollie had said, the tree twitched. Twice. Up at the top. As Sir Seth continued to stare, the tree twitched two more times. And once more after that. He slowly pulled out his sword. That witchy old tree had quite an eerie twitch in its top.

"There!" Sir Ollie shouted into the gloom. "Did you see that, Sir Seth? It's a good thing those dumb bumbleberries only gnawed off the end of El Gonzo. I might be needing him now."

"By golly, Sir Ollie, good work!" Sir Seth congratulated him. "Let's sneak up and have a closer look. But be careful. You don't want to end up wearing a weevil."

With rubbery knees and swords at the ready, the two fearless knights crept warily toward the witchy tree. Already, they were fast finding out that High Dudgeon was a lot eerier and scarier than they had expected. And home suddenly seemed a long, long way away.

"Look out!" Sir Ollie shouted shrilly in a voice somewhere above High C, shoving Sir Seth and Shasta safely to one side as he did.

"What's up, Sir Ollie?" he started to say. Then Sir Seth saw what Sir Ollie had just seen. It was the most awful, most awesome of sights.

A paw print!

But not from just any old paw. This was the size of a full-grown rhinosaurus rex, with three long, pointy claws like you'd find at the back of crocodiles' jaws.

"Wha...what kind of knight-gnawing beast has a footprint like that?" Sir Ollie anxiously wanted to know.

"Well, let's have a look," Sir Seth said. He kneeled down and measured the print with the span of both hands. "Hmmmmm, looks like a saber-toothed sloth to me. It's the only thing I can think of that has claws that size."

Sir Ollie turned a lighter shade of white. "Yeah? A for-real saber-toothed sloth?"

"Don't worry, Sir Ollie," Sir Seth reassured him. "I know it looks sorta scary, but those saber-tooths are really kinda slow, y'know. And if we can't outrun them, we can always stun them with our trusty sloth-slaying swords."

"Gee, Sir Seth, I don't know. This place even gives

my goosebumps the shivers. Are you, uh...are you sure you want to keep going?"

Sir Seth looked at Sir Ollie in awe. "Keep going? Of course we'll keep going. We promised Lady Sheri-Sue Shrood we'd get her father's shoes. And you know how you feel when someone makes you a promise and then doesn't come through."

"Yeah," Sir Ollie had to admit.

"Well, do you want her to feel that way about you?"

"Heck, no."

"Besides, you're not afraid of something as totally unscary as a silly old saber-toothed sloth, are you, Sir Ollie?"

"Me? No way. Come on, Sir Seth, let's go!"

With their swords at the ready, they crept through the fog on the balls of their tinfoil feet to make sure they didn't step on a branch or snap a dry twig. Which was just about impossible to find—because there hadn't been a dry anything in High Dudgeon for over three thousand years.

The three of them edged cautiously forward, testing each footstep they took. Then Sir Ollie heard it. It was a sort of definite something that sounded a bit like a roar or maybe a yawn. But whatever it was, it was up there in that twitching tree just ahead.

"Did...did you hear that?" Sir Ollie gasped, looking up. "There's something up there in that tree. Sounds like a yellow-eyed pit bullfrog to me."

Then, before either knight could shudder or stutter or speak, an ominous voice with a tongue-tangling lisp drifted down from the top of the tree.

"Don't be tho thilly," the voice said with a yawn. "Pit bullfrogth only come out at night."

The two brave knights jumped two feet straight up in the air, then passed Shasta on their way down.

"Who...who are you?" Sir Seth spluttered.

"That'th what I wuth about to athk you," the voice said, still out of sight. "Who are you...and what bringth you all the way up here to High Dudgeon?"

"Uh, who...who are *you*?" Sir Ollie stuttered.

"Who. Who. Who," the voice said with a snickering snuffle. "You thound like a couple of thilly old owlth.

But you didn't anther my quethtion...What bringth you here? And what do you want?"

With a busy rustling and bustling of leaves, the branches slowly parted, revealing an incredibly hairy, unbelievably scary saber-toothed sloth about four inches in front of Sir Ollie's knightly young nose!

"Aha! There you are," the upside-down sloth said around its frightening saber-toothed tusks as it put out a welcoming paw. "Hey, welcome to High Dudgeon, cuthin..."

But before the sloth could utter another word, Sir Ollie swung what was left of El Gonzo. "Quick, Sir Seth! Run for it! It's one of those knight-eating saber-toothed sloths!"

Fortunately, the sloth saw the sword coming and—although sloths are usually unbelievably slow—quickly ducked back into the tree before any damage was done. After a moment, a sad-sounding voice drifted down from somewhere inside the tree.

"Hey! Cool it, cuthin. I've never eaten a knight in my life. Heck, I don't even thcratch fleath," the sloth said, quite upset by the thought. "Now, put down your thordth and let'th talk, before thumbody around here geth hurt."

"Uh...sorry," Sir Seth said slowly. "It's okay. Come on back down. Let's talk."

Sir Seth and Sir Ollie and Shasta just stood there, stunned, too dazed and amazed to be scared. For there, upside down, right in front of their noses, hung an actual, factual, hairy old, really-not-so-scary old saber-toothed sloth that was not only real—it could actually talk! In English, not Slothish. But even more amazing than that, it had just called them its *cousins*!

"Sorry if we scared you," Sir Seth said and put out his hand. "I'm Sir Seth Thistlethwaite, at your service. And this is my friend Sir Ollie Everghettz."

The sloth sighed as it dropped down to the ground.

"Well, that's a little more like it. Glad to meet you, too," it said, heartily shaking Sir Seth's hand and rumpling Shasta's ears.

"Uh, sorry about the sword." Sir Ollie blushed now that he could plainly see how chummy a saber-toothed sloth could actually be. "But your saber-toothed teeth are so knee-knockingly scary, I guess I swung my sword before I could think."

"You mean theeth?" the sloth said as it reached up and removed its two long saber-toothed fangs.

"They're not real!?" exclaimed both knights together.

"Nope! You like 'em?" the sloth said emphatically. "I made them one day from the trunk of an elephant tree to make me look as scary as scary can be—because, y'see, when you're as slow-goin' as me, you've got to do something to scare all the weezils and wombats and werewolves away. Or you'd never make it through your first day in here."

"Werewolves?" Sir Ollie echoed. "Y'mean, there are werewolves in here, too, Mister Sloth?"

The sloth shrugged. "Well, first they *were* wolves, then they were *were*wolves. But I'm not sure what they are now. Oh, by the way, I'm not 'Mister Sloth.' My name's Edith-Anne."

"You're a girl!" Sir Seth and Sir Ollie gasped together.

She stared at them, amazed. "Well, yeah. With a name like Edith-Anne, what else would I be?"

"Sorry," the two knights said rather sheepishly.

Edith-Anne smiled a fetchingly saberless smile. "Hey, no problem. Now tell me, what brings you up here to High Dudgeon? You're the first tourists we've had here in three thousand years."

Sir Seth straightened. "Have you heard of Prince Quincy of Poxley?"

She jerked at the mere mention of the name. "The Prince of Poxley? Well, I might know that name," she said guardedly. "Why do you ask?"

Sir Seth decided to tell Edith-Anne the entire story. "...then the prince snuck down into Southernmost Thatchwych and stole Sir Shawn Shrood's magical truth-saying, soothsaying shoes from the castle. So Sir Ollie and I have come up here to get them and take them back to Lady Sheri-Sue."

"Ah, so I see," the sloth said slowly, thinking about their story.

"Well, can you tell us how to get to Poxley Castle?" Sir Ollie asked anxiously.

Edith-Anne looked at him for a long time before

answering. "Yep. That's the easy part. But, Ollie, I really don't think you know what you're asking."

She let go of the branch and pointed forlornly up into the gloom. "Y'see, to get to the prince's castle, you've got to go way, way up to the very top of High Dudgeon, cuzzin, where the fog is so thick you sometimes can't see three feet in front of your face. And when you get there, the whole place is crawling with bat dogs and bog frogs and spiders the size of horses. It's an awful, creepy old place. Are you really, really sure you want to go there?"

Sir Seth looked straight into Edith-Anne's eyes. "Yes. We promised Lady Sheri-Sue Shrood we'd get her father's shoes! And a promise is a promise, no matter what."

"Okay, cuzzins, suit yourselves," Edith-Anne said with a shrug and a three-second sigh. "But I sure hope you guys know how to fly."

"Fly?" Sir Ollie gasped, looking nervously at Sir Seth.

"Fly?" Sir Seth echoed, looking at Sir Ollie.

"Yeah. Fly. You know, like up in the sky," Edith-Anne said with a smile. "You weren't thinking of walking all the way to Poxley Castle, were you? That's a looooong way to walk, cuzzin. C'mon, flying is really, really easy. I'll show you how."

Sir Seth looked over at Shasta. "Okay...but you'll have to teach my horse how to fly, too."

Edith-Anne's eyes almost popped out of their sockets. "Your what?" she shouted about as excitedly as sloths ever get. "You brought a horse in here with you?"

"Yeah. My horse comes with us wherever we go. That's her over there," Sir Seth said, pointing to Shasta. "Looks like she's digging up something she found in the ground."

Edith-Anne's eyes were nicely getting back into their sockets, but when she saw Shasta, they nearly popped out all over again. "Oh, no! That's not a horse...it's a dog. And what's worse, your dog just dug up a bog runner's house."

"Uh, what's a bog runner?" Sir Ollie immediately wanted to know.

"You're about to find out in a minute," Edith-Anne said seriously. "Bog runners are the yabbering, blabbering big-mouths around here. They hide in holes they dig in the bog and hurry and scurry all over High Dudgeon, shoving their long brown noses into places they don't belong. And the minute they have juicy new news to blabber about, they head straight to the castle to tell pukey Prince Quincy and get their wormy reward. So, cuzzins, we've got to get outta here. And get outta here fast."

Without another word, Edith-Anne dashed over where Shasta was still excitedly nosing and digging around.

"Come on, cuzzin," she said, pulling on Shasta's collar.

But Shasta dug in her heels and simply wouldn't be budged. She was having far too much fun to worry about hurrying anywhere.

Then, in a flurry and a busy brown blur, the ground all around them was instantly awash and awhirl with a million—or perhaps even more than a billion—yabbering, blabbering bog runners. Dashing in circles like toy trains on a track, they hurried and scurried to be first to tell the prince that three strangely dressed strangers had just entered High Dudgeon—along with a saber-toothed sloth that could talk!

"Oh, oh...now we're really in trouble," Edith-Anne said in a no-nonsense way, as she tried once again to pull Shasta away. But Shasta, as knight's horses are all trained to do, was busily wagging her tail and sniffing each bog runner as it ran by.

"Shasta! Come here, girl. Treat time!" Sir Seth called—which usually meant he had some meatloaf sandwich to spare. It was much better than sniffing a bunch of smelly old bog runners any day.

"Okay, everybody, over here. Gather round quick," Edith-Anne said, as she unscrewed the end of one of her saber-toothed teeth and poured some glittery golden liquid into one paw.

"Quick, quick, quick. Take a lick," she said, offering her paw to the knights. "We've got to get up there to Poxley Castle fast, before all these gabbing gossips can tell Prince Quincy you're here."

"Uh, what is this stuff?" Sir Ollie wanted to know.

"Hey, hey, you're gonna love it, cuzzin!" Edith-Anne said with a huge smile. "It's my magical Sloth Broth. Watch this. You take a quick lick, then hang on to your hat. Because when you do, you'll find you're suddenly able to...fly!"

Gaily garbed in his cheerful graveyard gray cape and matching bat-plumed black hat, the poxy Prince Quincy of Poxley greeted the new day with a long, roaring yawn. Then, stroking Sam and Ella—his pair of paunchy pet rats—on their greedy little, beady-eyed heads, he stumbled, still half-asleep, toward the tightly shut windows at the foot of his bed. Then he glanced up at the clock.

"Ah, my vile little vixens. Dear, deary me, just look at the time. It's past nine! The day is half-done before it's even begun," he whispered to the two fawning faces looking back up at him. "And there's so much sooth to be said before two."

In a bit of a snit, the prince swung open the tightly shut shutters and peered out onto High Dudgeon, immediately brightening as he drank in the day.

"Ah, just as I'd hoped...another fabulously funereal day in every imaginable way, bathed in two hundred glorious shades of gray. And look over there, at those wondrous, thunderous storm clouds shrouded in lightning-splashed, tornado-lashed mist. Everywhere one looks, one sees Mother Nature at her breathtaking best. It fairly makes you want to break into a dirge, does it not?"

The two fat, scaredy-cat rats vigorously agreed with their usual pointy-toothed grins.

Then the thought struck him—here it was, past nine, and he hadn't yet had a single selfish thought or a nasty idea to brighten or otherwise lighten his way through the fast-disappearing day.

"And now, my putrid little pets," the prince said, as he dropped Sam and Ella on their heads on the bed, "it's time to try on my magical soothsaying shoes. There's so much sooth to be said about me today, I barely know where to begin."

The prince breezed across the room to the ornate gold-and-red chest he had hidden in his closet. And there, nestled safely inside, were the red silk soothsaying shoes that Sir Seth and Sir Ollie were sworn, on their honor, to save.

With a trembling hand and a kind of catch in his laugh, Prince Quincy reached down and tenderly stroked the satiny shoes. "At last, my plump little dumplings, I am about to become all those yummy things that Mummy said I would be—such as a laudable, applaudable leader, idolized and adored by all my hordes of loyal, loving subjects throughout the land. So let us see what sort of sooth these shoes are capable of creating for me, shall we?" he eagerly asked, holding up the red shoes. "Well, come along, come along. Speak up. What's the matter? Has the cat got your tongues?"

However, the two roly-poly rodents simply sat where they were and gawked in open-mouthed awe at the prince—mainly because they were, quite plainly, rats that couldn't understand a single word Prince Quincy said. But fortunately for Sam and Ella, the prince stepped in and saved the day by, once again, answering his own question.

"Aha! I've just had another of my frightfully insightful ideas! I think we should begin today's soothsaying by introducing some new sooth about me. Don't you agree?"

Now, although Sam and Ella were unable to utter a single syllable of their own—and didn't understand a thing the prince said—they had become very, very good at nodding their heads very, very vigorously whenever he asked them a question. Which is one of the reasons they were so very, very well fed. Because if the prince had but one kind streak, it was an unfailing fondness for people, or rats, or anything else that completely agreed with everything he said.

Prince Quincy walked over and admired himself in the mirror. "Now, then, let me see...what sort of sooth shall I start spreading about poor, poor misunderstood little me? Well, I suppose I could—and I probably should—begin

by telling everybody about my boundless generosity."
he thought out loud, as he whirled with a flourish to face Sam and Ella.

Sam and Ella nearly wore out their necks nodding.

"What's this?" he boomed in a bellow so frighteningly gruff and abrupt it blew the two rats right off all eight of their feet. "How dare you agree! Why, everyone, everywhere, already knows of my wondrous good nature and exemplary good deeds. So why should we waste any sooth by telling them things that they already know?"

Sam and Ella nearly wore out their necks shaking their heads in agreement.

"Ah, but, my beady-eyed little friends, with these magical soothsaying shoes on my feet, I can tell anybody anything—anything at all—and they'll be obliged to believe it. Because, as we well know, these soothsayer's shoes instantly turn everything I say into the beautiful, indisputable truth."

He paused grandly to let it sink in.

"Think of it, my repulsive little pets. Do you realize what this means? With these amazing soothsayer's shoes on my feet, I can convince people that I'm anyone I've ever wanted to be!"

If you thought that things in High Dudgeon were already bad, the only thing that could possibly make everything worse was a High Dudgeon where everybody believed everything Prince Quincy said!

A bad day just doesn't get any badder than that!

5 VERY SCARY Poxley Castle

Sir Seth gasped in open-mouthed awe as he rose slowly up, up, up past the tips and the tops of the tall tumbledown trees—then up and up and up some more until he was soaring through the soft, gray fluffy-wuffy nothingness of a low-flying cloud.

"Hey, Edith-Anne!" he shouted with a shudder. "Help! I don't think flying is one of the things I do best."

"I'm right beside you, cuzzin," the sloth's soothing voice assured him from somewhere nearby.

Sir Seth looked around but couldn't see a thing. "Uh, quick! How do you steer up here?"

Just then, Sir Ollie went breezing by, with his upside-down side definitely up. His eyes were the size of a polar bear's paws.

He was quickly followed by Shasta, who was as completely confused as she'd ever been—wondering how she could suddenly be taller than a tumbledown tree.

"Sorry, Sir Seth," Edith-Anne's assuring voice said from somewhere close by. "I didn't have time to show you down there, but flying is easy—you just hold out your arms like the wings on a plane, then point your feet down and hold them together. That'll keep you going in a straight line. And next thing you know, you'll be flitting all over the sky like a lark."

Sir Seth did as she suggested, and almost at once, his downside stayed down and his upside stayed up.

Then, in a wink, before he could think, he flew out of the swirling gray cloud—and gasped right out loud. For there, three thousand feet below, sprawling in fifty different colors of gray, lay soggy old, boggy old High Dudgeon—looking drearily back up at him.

Edith-Anne glided up beside him, her long hair flapping in the wind. "See how easy it is? I knew you could do it. Now, see that creepy black castle, way, way over there by that stream, looking like a fly on a bowl of ice cream?"

"Yeah."

"Well, guess what, cuzzin? That's Poxley Castle."

Sir Seth stared down where Edith-Anne was pointing. He couldn't have imagined a worse place if someone had said to him right there and right then: "Sir Seth, I want you to think of the double-uckiest place you can imagine—where decaying old mummies and even zombies won't go. Then multiply that awfulness by three thousand and two. And that's what Prince Quincy calls home!"

"Hey, Sir Seth, lookit this!" Sir Ollie interrupted

as he suddenly went flying by, then swooped straight up into a loop. "I'm an F-18. Flying is just too, too cool to be true!"

Sir Ollie then came gliding up beside them and saw the castle for the first time. "Oh, yuck! Is that Poxley Castle?"

"Yep," Edith-Anne confirmed. "How do you like it so far?"

"It looks like a good place not to go. And look over there! All those little brown bugs are going there too."

"Little brown bugs?" Edith-Anne gasped. "What little brown bugs?"

Then she saw them.

"Uh-oh...we have problems. Those little brown bugs aren't little brown bugs, cuzzins. They're those spying, prying bog runners that Shasta dug up."

"And they're heading straight for the castle!" Sir Seth shuddered.

"To tell the prince that we're here!" Ollie uttered in shock.

"Follow me, cuzzins!" Edith-Anne called over one shoulder. "We'll have to dive if we want to get there first. This is gonna be close."

And with that, Edith-Anne rolled over into a nosedive, heading almost straight down.

Sir Seth did his best to keep up, but she was traveling much, much too fast. Then he took a quick look around—and realized with a frown that Sir Ollie and Shasta were nowhere to be found. But down, down, down he flew, desperately trying to keep up with Edith-Anne.

The next thing he knew, they were zigging and zagging at roughly warp speed about a foot and a half above the gray blur of the ground. Still sticking to her unwavering course to the castle, Edith-Anne didn't let anything get in her way or slow her down.

The two of them zoomed through the outstretched arms of a tumbledown tree, then dropped down until they were an inch and a half from the ground, weaving their way through dense thickets of spiny bat-bramble bushes that hung in a Frankensteinian fog over an inky blackwater bog that's infested, so it's said, with giant dog-eating bog frogs.

Then, without any warning whatever, Edith-Anne stopped almost dead in mid-flight, sending Sir Seth cartwheeling in a tumbling jumble of bashed knees and bruised nose and toes into a happily napping umbrella bush, which roused itself briefly and grumped, then went back to its dreams of sunshine, no doubt.

"Uh, sorry, cuzzin," Edith-Anne whispered as she brushed most of the mud from Sir Seth's knees, nose, and clothes. "We're almost there, but I'm afraid I have some bad news...I just lost all my Sloth Broth on the way down. We'll have to go the rest of the way on foot."

"Not without Sir Ollie and Shasta, we won't!" Sir Seth said firmly, refusing to budge.

"No problem, cuzzin." The sloth smiled. "But you'd better duck or you're gonna get goosed—'cause here they come now."

Sir Seth turned just in time to see Sir Ollie go streaking by as though he'd just been shot out of a cannon—feet first, upside down, and about a foot and a half from the ground—followed by a still wide-eyed Shasta, whose attempt at flying was even awfuler than Sir Ollie's.

"Hey, Edith-Anne!" Sir Ollie cried as he breezed by, "Flying is fun, but you forgot to tell me one thing—how do I stop?"

"Uh-oh, this doesn't look good..." Edith-Anne sighed and closed her eyes.

Before she could tell him to go around one more time, Sir Ollie and Shasta zoomed up into a climb—then stalled and came tumbling down, shedding a shower of shiny bits of aluminum foil and armor all the way down. They landed in a jumbled head-over-heels-and-paws heap right on top of—what else?—the slumbering umbrella bush, which had just gone back to sleep.

Sir Seth ran over to Sir Ollie and Shasta. "Are you guys okay?"

"I think so," Sir Ollie said slowly, almost afraid to find out.

"Your friend and your dog are both fine. But what about me?" a voice nearby suddenly wanted to know.

Sir Seth looked quickly around in a complete circle. But no one was there. "Who said that?"

"Said what?" Sir Ollie asked, still gathering his wits.

"I just heard a voice."

Edith-Anne immediately perked up. "A voice? What did it say?"

"It just said, 'What about me?'"

"Right. That's exactly what I said," the voice said again.

"Oh, no, it's Hugh." Edith-Anne groaned and sat down with a thud.

It was Sir Ollie's turn to turn all the way around. "Hugh? Who's Hugh?"

"Hugh the Yew. The non-stop talking tree."

"A talking tree?" Sir Seth perked up. "I didn't know trees could talk."

"Talk!" Edith-Anne almost shouted. "Hugh never shuts up. I just wish that for once, he'd have something interesting to say."

"And you're just a silly old sloth that doesn't know its ups from its downs," Hugh huffed, somewhat hurt. "Y'see, here in High Dudgeon, I don't get many chances to chat. No one ever drops by for a friendly 'yew hoo' or 'how do yew do,'" the tree shrugged sort of sadly.

"Don't worry about me. I can see you're in a hurry to be on your way. But before you go, perhaps you should know...I know a secret way you can get into the castle."

Then, as quick as a wink, before you could blink—which is really quite quick for a sloth that usually moves about as quickly as a moth—Edith-Anne flew to the yew with a great big, chummy grin.

"You do?"

"Do what?" Hugh the Yew said, suddenly quite coy.

"You said you know of a secret way into the castle," Edith-Anne reminded him.

"Oh? Did I?" Hugh was enjoying the conversation so much he didn't want it ever to end. "Maybe I did. Maybe I didn't."

Edith-Anne gave Hugh a great big hug. "C'mon, Hughie, you great big, wonderful old yew, you. Share your secret with your friends."

"With my friends?" Hugh snorted. "Surely you don't mean you, do you?"

Edith-Anne had to think fast. "I was talking about all your friends down in Southernmost Thatchwych—or haven't you heard the news?"

"News? What news?" Hugh perked up immediately.

"Ohhhhh, nothing much," Edith-Anne began. "Just that creepy old Prince Quincy sent someone down there to steal the soothsayer's shoes."

"He did? Oh deary me," Hugh snorted angrily.

Edith-Anne leaned even closer, whispering. "And these Mighty Knights have come all the way here to get the shoes back. Now will you tell them how to get into the castle?"

The yew was so shocked that for once he could hardly talk. "Oh, deary me, yes. I'm sure I can trust my secret with two gallant knights such as these."

"Mister Yew, I promise you your secret will be safe with us," Sir Ollie said solemnly.

"Our word is our word," Sir Seth agreed. "And a word you can trust."

"I'm sure it is. Well, now. Let me see..." Hugh the Yew sighed, scratching his tousled head slowly, as yews tend to do when they're trying to think—because thinking is something a yew doesn't do as such, very much. "You could try to sneak through the laundry room door. No, no, it's always locked until four. Well, perhaps you could..."

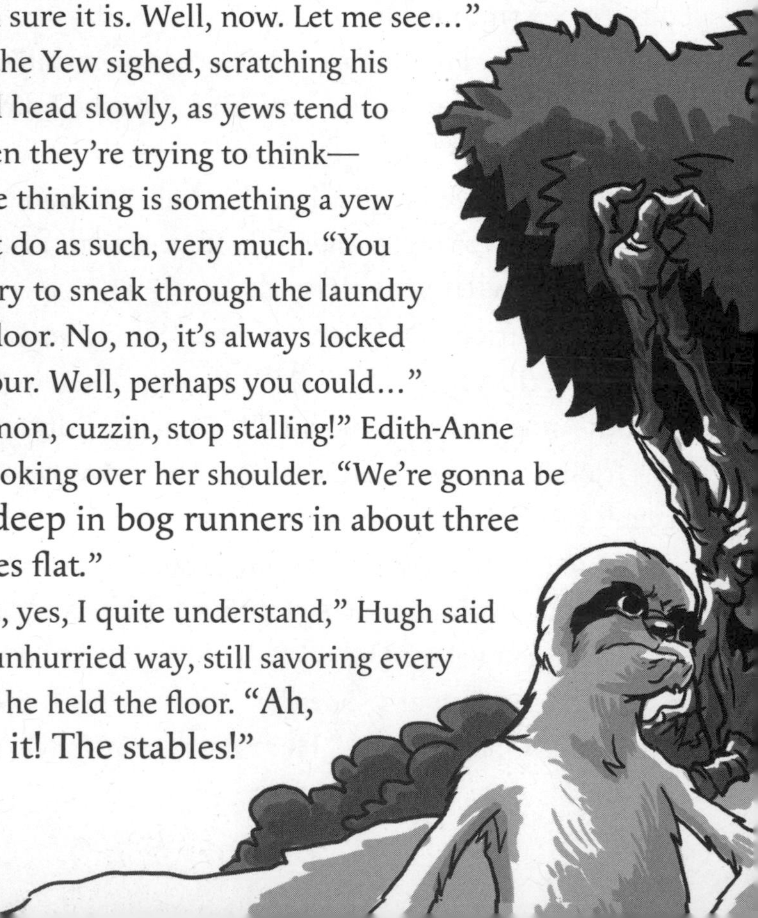

"C'mon, cuzzin, stop stalling!" Edith-Anne said, looking over her shoulder. "We're gonna be knee-deep in bog runners in about three minutes flat."

"Yes, yes, I quite understand," Hugh said in his unhurried way, still savoring every second he held the floor. "Ah, I have it! The stables!"

"What stables?" Sir Ollie urged him excitedly.

"The stables at the Horse Guards Palace, of course!" Hugh the Yew said about as excitedly as you've ever seen a yew get.

"What happens at the stables?" Sir Seth said, still confused.

Hugh leaned down and whispered into Sir Seth's ear in case someone unsavory was near who might also hear. "If you hurry, you can get to the Horse Palace just as the King's Kung Fu Fusiliers are changing the guard," Hugh said, still excitedly. "When the gate opens, the guards will all be so busy changing, you can simply ride in on your horse, disguised, of course, as two of the King's Kung Fu Fusiliers."

"On my...horse?" Sir Seth echoed.

"Yes, yes, of course on your horse—unless, of course, you don't have a horse," the tree said, surprised. "You do have a horse, don't you? I thought all knights rode horses wherever they went."

"Uh, what's a fusilier?" Sir Ollie wanted to know.

"Ah, silly me," Hugh said, somewhat embarrassed. "They're the kingdom's special forces. They're good at kung fu and everything else they do—and luckily for you, they all ride horses. You'll find two King's Kung Fu Fusilier's uniforms trying to dry on that tree just behind me. They've been there for two hundred years, but in all this rain, nothing will ever get dry, I'm afraid."

"Oh, thank you, thank you, Mister Yew—" Sir Ollie started to say.

"You can come back and thank me some other time," the yew suggested. "Right now, you'd better hurry if you want to get to the palace in time."

"He's right, cuzzins," Edith-Anne urgently agreed. "We've got to get going."

They all scurried around behind Hugh, and sure enough, just as he said, two King's Kung Fu Fusilier's uniforms sagged forlornly in the dreary High Dudgeon drizzle, trying desperately to get dry.

But as luck would have it, two hundred years of hanging out there in the unending rain had shrunk them down to the same size as a ten-year-old knight!

"Wow!" Sir Ollie gasped when he saw them. "Look at all those gold badges and medals and stuff. This is just too, too totally cool to be true."

He took down one of the uniforms and held it up to his chest. "Well, what do you think? Do I look like a King's Kung Fu Fusilier—or what?"

"You look great, cuzzin," Edith-Anne sighed. "But we've got a problem."

"What kind of a problem?"

Edith-Anne shrugged. "Do the math."

"Math?" Sir Seth and Sir Ollie shuddered at the word. "What math?"

Edith-Anne shrugged again. "Count the uniforms."

Sir Seth looked at Sir Ollie. And Sir Ollie looked at Sir Seth. "Uh...two."

"Right. Now count the knights."

"Uh...two."

"Right. Now count the horses," Edith-Anne sighed.

"Ooops."

"That's right. We've got two knights, one horse, and a sloth."

Sir Seth turned as white as Upper Thatchwychian snow. "Uh-oh. That is a problem."

But then, as Mighty Knights are somehow able to do, Sir Seth and Sir Ollie thought the exact same thought at the very same moment. Then, together as one, they turned to face Edith-Anne—to announce the bad news.

For less than a sixth of a second or so, Edith-Anne stood there staring back at them. Then the same shocking knightly thought occurred to her, too.

"Wait a minute," she gasped, backing up in horror. "You want me to be a horse? Sorry, cuzzins. My arms are too long, my tail is too short, and I don't know how to prance or to snort. You'll just have to find a horse somewhere else."

Sir Seth put his arm around her. "Y'know, I was thinking...when we get back to Thatchwych, if Sir Ollie and I told King Philip Fluster the Fourth how much you helped us bring back the soothsayer's shoes, he might just want to make you a Mighty Knight, too."

"Me? A Mighty Knight?" Edith-Anne gasped at the thought. "Do you think he would?"

Sir Seth shrugged. "He could. But remember, a Mighty Knight never says no. Not even when it comes to being a horse."

"But horses don't hang upside down from a tree."

Sir Seth smiled up at her. "Sir Edith-Anne could. Can you?"

Edith-Anne knew when she was trapped. "Okay, cuzzin, hop on."

Then, to remind them the time for chitchat was well and truly over, from the not-so-distant distance came the unmistakable sound of a herd—or a horde—of bog runners closing in on the castle.

"I knew this would happen if we didn't stop yappin'," Edith-Anne said quickly. "Now we've really gotta go!"

With that, the two disguised knights took the reins of their horses and started up the long shadowy pathway that snaked through the tangle of brambles and bat bogs all the way up to the towering turrets of Poxley Castle. And the nearer they drew, the eerier and scarier it became.

The dreary gray day seemed to grow even darker. And drearier. And eerier. Then everything grew even darker and eerier and drearier than that.

The sky was heavy with swirling gray clouds painted with nightmarish faces that swooped down all around them like hosts of low-flying ghosts—whispering what sounded like hollow-voiced moanings and groanings and warnings:

"GO NO FARTHER. GO BA-A-A-ACK WHILE YOU STILL CAN."

"Did you hear that?" Sir Ollie suddenly said, stopping dead in his tracks. "I think I just heard my mom call me for lunch."

"Not scared, are you, cuzzin?" Edith-Anne teased him.

"M-m-me? Nope. It's just when my mom calls me, I gotta go."

"Well, then, let's go—all the way to the castle."

Without saying another word, the four of them made their way up the long, steep hill—each lost in thought, wondering what would happen when they reached the castle.

Still, on they went. And on. And on. Until they came to a clearing where, with a heart-jabbing jolt, it stood—dark and stark and for real. Poxley Castle itself. Looming up into the gloom for forty-four stories. Or so it seemed. In fact, the castle was suddenly so creepily close, Sir Ollie was sure he saw a bat fly out of one of the upstairs windows—in the daytime!

"I wonder how long it took someone to paint the whole castle black like that?" Sir Seth wondered, looking almost straight up.

"Or why they would want to," Sir Ollie added.

"Never mind that," Edith-Anne whispered. "Start wondering where we can find the stables instead."

But Sir Seth was still in awe of the castle. "How are we gonna find a pair of shoes in a castle this big?" he wondered out loud, still looking up. "It could take us **forever**. Maybe even longer than that."

"How are we gonna find the gate to the Horse Guards Palace, is what I want to know. Let's try around this corner."

Slowly, and cautiously as four little mice, they edged their way around the corner of the castle. Then, out of nowhere, a woman's voice said:

"Halt!"

Then said nothing more.

"**Who's there?**" Sir Ollie wanted to know.

"That's supposed to be my next question to you," the voice said, somewhat upset. "Now we'll have to go back to the beginning and start all over again. Are you ready?"

"Uh...ready," Sir Seth said rather unsurely.

"Good. Then, as I said before...Halt!"

Sir Seth whirled around in a complete circle, without seeing anyone at all.

"Where are you?" he finally asked.

"I'm right beside you," the voice said even closer than before. "Can't you hear me?"

"I can hear you fine," Sir Seth said, still quite confused. "But why can't I see you?"

"You can't see me, you see, because I'm a voice," the voice said impatiently, as though talking to a very young child. "And who's ever heard of anyone seeing a voice? Voices exist strictly for hearing—or haven't you heard?"

Sir Seth whispered to Edith-Anne, "Who is she?"

"It's Joyce," she sighed. "First it was Hugh the Yew, and now we have Joyce the Voice."

"Who's Joyce the Voice?"

"She's one of the prince's invisible spies. He has voices like Joyce's in every corner of the castle. They're even bigger blabbermouths than those bog runners—because when you think about it, blabbering is all you can do if all you are is a voice."

"So now that you know who I am," Joyce sniffed with disdain, "Just who, may I ask, are you?"

"Could we talk this over inside the castle, where it's dry?" Edith-Anne suggested with her best chumsy-wumsy smile. "Where would we find the stable gate?"

"Oh! How silly of me," Joyce exclaimed. "You must be the new fusiliers, here for the changing of the guard.

We've been expecting you. Please, come with me. I'll get your horses some oats."

"Oats?" Edith-Anne asked nervously.

"Yes, of course," Joyce the Voice said firmly. "All horses eat oats, don't they?"

"Oh, some do. But most of us prefer ju-jubes instead."

"Ju-jubes? How very odd. I'll see if we've got any. In the meantime, I'll alert the Captain of the Guard that you're here. You can enter the castle through the stables gate over there."

Sir Seth excitedly nudged Sir Ollie without saying a word. Then, as calmly and casually as he could possibly walk, Sir Seth led his horse, Shasta, straight through the gate, then through the courtyard past all the prancing Horse Guards and King's Kung Fu Fusiliers, right into the stables—as easy as one, two, three, four, shut the door.

Sir Seth whirled around, and there were Sir Ollie and Edith-Anne, looking even more surprised than he and Shasta.

"Can you buhhhhlieve it?"

"This is just too, too good to be true," Sir Ollie laughed and slapped Sir Seth on the shoulder. "I can't believe how easy it was."

Thanks to their friend Hugh the Yew, they were suddenly—all of them—inside the castle!

6 The Eerie, Cheery GHOST King

The ancient stable door slammed shut behind them with a thunderous, dust-swirling roar. Sir Seth looked at Sir Ollie and swallowed hard.

"Well, we wanted to get inside the castle. And here we are, inside the castle. That's for sure."

Of that, there wasn't a doubt. However, now that they were in, the new problem was...there was no way to get out.

"Well, this is what we wanted," Edith-Anne's voice echoed, as she nervously looked around in the gloom. "And here we are. But just look at this room. Has the prince never heard of a broom?"

Her eyes darted quickly up and down the frightful straw-strewn stables at row upon row of dark, empty stalls, without so much as a window in sight to let in some fresh air and light.

"It sure is dark in here," Sir Ollie noted out loud. "So what do we do now?"

"I'm not sure," Sir Seth had to admit, looking up at the heavy castle door. "But I know one thing for sure—there won't be any bog runners coming through that door."

"Come on, let's get out of here," Edith-Anne suggested nervously, "before Joyce gets back with those oats."

"And go where?" Sir Seth said, still looking around. "I don't know where we are now."

"And trying to find the soothsayer's shoes in here will be like trying to find a flea in a fir tree," Edith-Anne added, also looking around.

"Nawwwww, it'll be easy," Sir Ollie said.

Sir Seth and Edith-Anne both looked at Sir Ollie. "Yeah? And just what makes you think so?"

"I don't think so. I know so," Sir Ollie said with a grin. "They'll be in the bedroom. That's where my shoes are each morning when I'm getting dressed."

"Of course!" Sir Seth said excitedly, giving him a knightly high-five. "By golly, Sir Ollie, that's exactly where they are. And bedrooms are always on the top floor. Right?"

Even Shasta stopped sniffing long enough to woof and wag with excitement.

"Right you are, cuzzin," Edith-Anne agreed. "So what are we waiting for? Let's see if we can find another door out of this room."

Sir Seth and Sir Ollie removed their fusilier uniforms, and the four of them crept quickly around the dimly lit stable until they came to the only other door they could find. It was a huge, incredibly heavy door, taller than all four of them standing on each other's shoulders—with a rusty metal latch, a keyhole the size of your fist, and huge rusty hinges that looked as though they hadn't been oiled since Sir Seth was a tot.

"Come on, Sir Ollie, give me a boost," Sir Seth said, looking up at the latch.

Sir Ollie put his hands together, making them into a "booster," the way Sir Seth did when he wanted to get cherries from the tree at the end of the yard. Sir Seth put one foot in the booster, then Sir Ollie oomphed him easily up to the latch. He grasped the latch in both hands, then pushed down with both thumbs as hard as he could. But the rusty old latch just wouldn't budge.

However, in case you've forgotten, Sir Seth is a Mighty Knight of Right & Honor. Which means he never gives up. So he tried once again, just a little bit harder. Then again, just a little bit harder than that. Then harder and harder until his thumbs turned white. But that stubborn old latch just wouldn't budge.

"We gotta get some oil," Sir Seth sighed and sagged slightly, temporarily stumped.

"Oil?" Sir Ollie said, looking around quickly.

"Oil?" Edith-Anne echoed. "Cuzzin, we're not gonna find much oil in a stable. But I'll have a look around..."

Edith-Anne immediately disappeared into the gray gloom of the room, feeling her way with her shins, so it seemed, bumping and thumping her knees, nose, and toes in the darkness and making more noise than thirty-six sloths ten times her size.

Finally, from out there, somewhere in the cobwebs and shadows, she shouted out a happy discovery. "I didn't find any oil, cuzzins. But I found a nice sledgehammer instead." Then, like a gray shark, Edith-Anne emerged from the dark, excitedly holding a huge hammer. "If this doesn't do it, nothing will."

Sir Seth took the hammer in both hands and gave the latch his frightfuliest, knightliest stare. Then he swung the hammer as hard as he could. And with a screeching, raspy complaint, the latch budged. Just a bit.

Not a lot.

But a little.

"It moved!" Sir Ollie announced at the top of his voice. "Hit it again!"

"Hey, cuzzin, keep down the noise," Edith-Anne whispered. "Everyone in the whole castle will know that we're here."

Sir Seth tried not to worry while he was hurrying, but it seemed he was moving in slow motion instead. He swung the hammer again and hit the latch dead on its head. And once more, just like before, the latch moved a bit. Sir Seth felt he was beginning to win.

He swung the sledge again and again, and each time the rusty old latch squawked and balked but moved just a bit more. Then, just as Sir Seth thought he had won, part of the latch suddenly snapped off and fell to the floor with a loud, heart-stopping crash.

"Oh, no! You almost had it. Try hitting it up from the bottom," Sir Ollie suggested in a loud whisper, the way nervous knights are sometimes able to do.

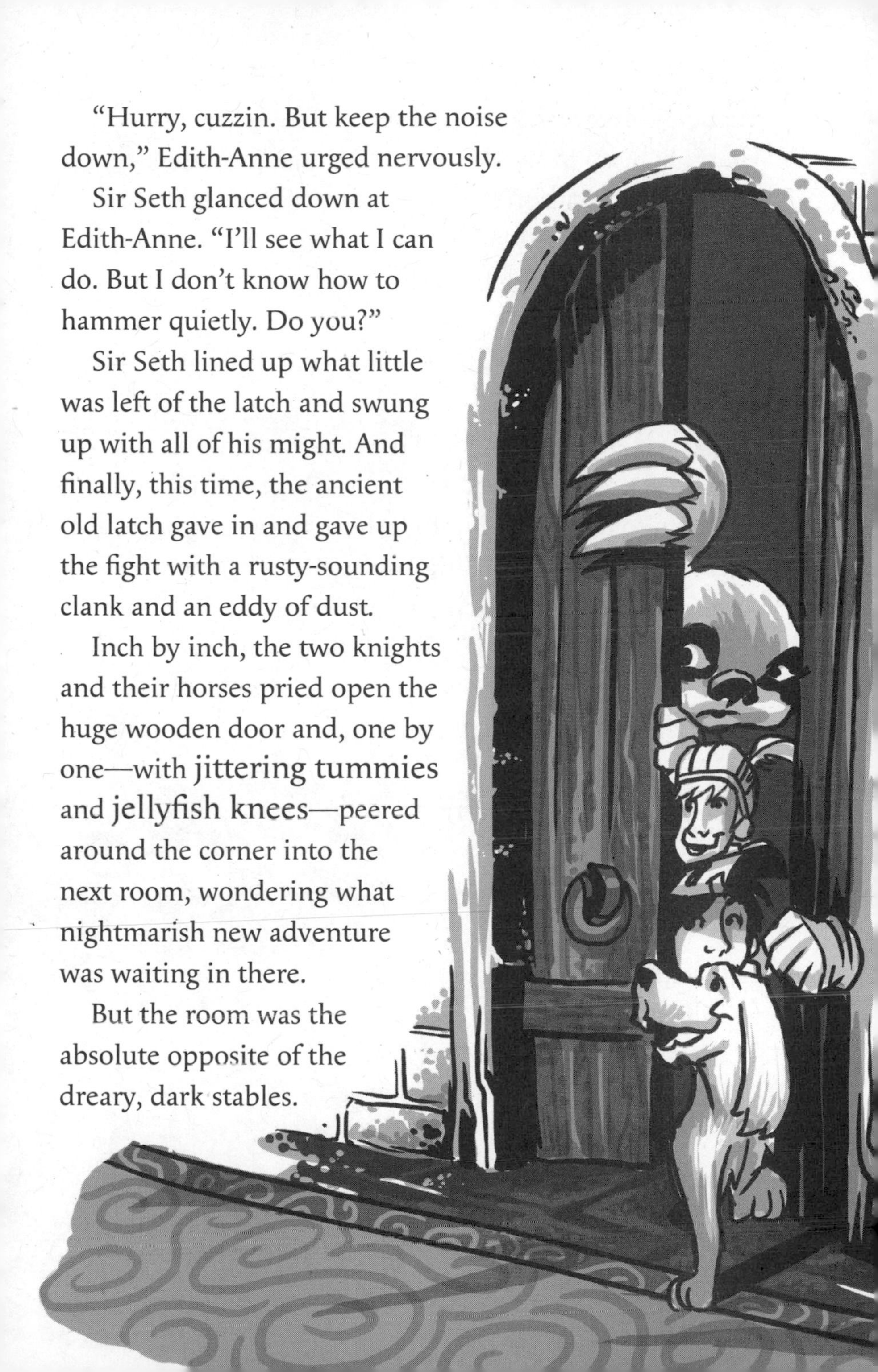

"Hurry, cuzzin. But keep the noise down," Edith-Anne urged nervously.

Sir Seth glanced down at Edith-Anne. "I'll see what I can do. But I don't know how to hammer quietly. Do you?"

Sir Seth lined up what little was left of the latch and swung up with all of his might. And finally, this time, the ancient old latch gave in and gave up the fight with a rusty-sounding clank and an eddy of dust.

Inch by inch, the two knights and their horses pried open the huge wooden door and, one by one—with jittering tummies and jellyfish knees—peered around the corner into the next room, wondering what nightmarish new adventure was waiting in there.

But the room was the absolute opposite of the dreary, dark stables.

Suddenly, everything was as breathtakingly white as wintry light on fresh-fallen snow. Neat tidy rows of white wooden benches sat in front of row upon row of white wooden wardrobes, where the prince and his horse-riding friends must surely have gathered when they were preparing to ride.

And best of all, despite the banging and clanging, there was no one in sight.

"Okay, follow me, men," Sir Seth whispered as loud as he could, as he entered the room where the light was suddenly so dazzlingly bright, it hurt his eyes trying to see.

"Follow me, who?" Edith-Anne whispered back.

"Ooops. Sorry, Edith-Anne. I meant to say, 'Follow me, everybody.' How's that?"

"Much better indeed!" a booming baritone voice said from somewhere nearby.

Edith-Anne stopped dead in her tracks. "Oh, no. Not another voice."

"I'm afraid so," the voice roared with laughter. "Allow me to introduce myself, if I may. I am Walter Poxley, the three-thousand-year-old ghost and your humble host while you're my guests here at Poxley Castle.

But please, my friends call me Jolly King Wally. I hope you'll do me the honor of doing the same."

"Uh, did you just say...ghost?" Sir Ollie suddenly wanted to know, backing into Sir Seth, who backed into Shasta, who backed into the wall.

"Yes, of course," King Wally said proudly from somewhere near Sir Ollie. "Many people become ghosts when they're finished being people. It's what you must do, if you want to stay here."

"You are Jolly King Wally... Poxley?" Sir Seth asked, with the same shiver as Sir Ollie's. "Your name is the same as the castle."

"Now, now...there's no need to be nervous, my fine fretting friends," King Wally chuckled warmly. "Please relax. It is a pleasure to have such brave young knights as yourselves as my guests. We don't get many visitors up here in High Dudgeon. So tell me... what brings you all the way up here?"

But before anyone could answer, Jolly King Wally walked right through the wall in a mostly ghostly, see-through sort of way, about two inches from where Sir Ollie was standing.

The moment they all saw him, both of the knights and both of their horses drew in their breath in a sort of group gasp. King Wally Poxley was, to be sure, everything that every king ought to be like. Every detail was just so incredibly and royally right. Without any doubt, he was the most magnificent monarch Sir Seth had ever seen. Or seen through.

He was breathtakingly attired—from the top of his jewel-crested gold crown all the way down to the tips of his gleaming black leather boots—in a long, rich red-and-gold velvet robe, with swirls of white curls tumbling down from his crown all around his flowing white beard. And as a finishing touch, he was richly endowed with warm, happy laughter and gentle Santa Claus eyes. Jolly King Wally was, without any doubt, the kingliest of kings.

Which immediately made Sir Seth wonder what someone as magnificent as King Wally was doing in a place as appalling as Poxley Castle.

"Sire," Sir Seth began, feeling his way for the right words, "I am Sir Seth Thistlethwaite and these are my friends Sir Ollie and Edith-Anne. We've come here at the request of Lady Sheri-Sue Shrood, the fair daughter of the soothsayer of Thatchwych, Sir Shawn Shrood."

"Yes, please go on," King Wally encouraged Sir Seth.

"Well, we've come to rescue Sir Shawn's soothsaying shoes and return them where they rightfully belong."

"As well you might, sir knight," King Wally heartily agreed. "But tell me, just how did Sir Shawn's shoes find their way up here to High Dudgeon, I wonder?"

Sir Seth took a deep breath, not sure what King Wally's reaction would be. "Well, um, I'm afraid it was Prince Quincy of Poxley, Sire. He had someone steal the shoes because he wants to use their mystical powers for himself."

Suddenly, Jolly King Wally wasn't so jolly at all.

"He did what!?" the king roared like rolling thunder that shook the chandeliers and blew the dust out from under the rugs all the way up to the forty-fourth floor. "Oh, when shall I ever be rid of this unending curse!"

"Um...did you say c-c-curse, sir?" Sir Ollie suddenly wanted to know.

"Yes, Sir Ollie, a curse. And it's the worst kind of curse, I'm afraid," the king said with a long weary sigh. "You probably don't know, but a long time ago—when I was alive and king of High Dudgeon—this was the most magnificent kingdom imaginable, bathed from morning till night in a soft yellow light, with trillions of tiny canaries warbling wherever you went. Sometimes with three or four—or even more—to a tree. And smiles were a part of the everyday art of simply being alive.

"Then one fine morning, a mysterious old man arrived from a faraway land, somewhere far east of these mountains. The only possessions he brought with him were the wisdom of ages and a creaky antique walking stick with the word 'Truth' carved on the handle.

"But while he was our guest here at Poxley Castle, someone stole the old man's antique walking stick in the hope it contained some magical, mystical powers. Of course, it did not. It was simply an old man's walking stick with the word 'Truth' carved on the handle.

"The old man was so distressed, he walked straight to the window, and raising both arms to the sky—and with a tear in his eye—he bid the sky to cloud over and cry, not drops of rain but tears of sadness and shame. And thus shall it remain. Until the good name of Poxley can be trusted again."

The king stopped and looked out the window.

"As you clearly can see, those tears have been raining steadily down on High Dudgeon for more than three thousand years. And try as this ghost might to set our name right, it seemed as each new Poxley came along, he did something that made the curse even worse. And now, you say my great-great-great-great-great-great-grandson, Quincy—the Prince of Poxley—has stolen Sir Shawn Shrood's soothsaying shoes because he believes they also contain some mystical, magical powers? It seems the good name of Poxley is doomed for the next three thousand years, wouldn't you say?"

"Gee, I hope not," Sir Ollie sighed.

"There must be something we can do to help Prince Quincy do something good," Sir Seth wondered out loud.

Then, at that exact moment in time, the beginning of an idea suddenly popped into Sir Seth's agile mind.

"Sire," he began slowly, as the idea gathered speed, "if somebody—such as Sir Ollie and me—could get the prince to return Sir Shawn's shoes, do you think that would help stop the rain, by making the name of Poxley a good one again?"

King Wally's mind began to race at the same pace as Sir Seth's. "Yes, Sir Seth! I believe that it could." Then he thought about it some more. "It's certainly worth a try. You know, as a knight, anything's possible if you try hard enough. Come along, follow me."

Then, without one more word, King Wally whirled and walked straight through the wall—as easily as though the wall hadn't been there at all—and disappeared right out of sight, leaving the two knights and their horses standing alone in the hall.

"What a neat trick," Sir Ollie said, putting his hand on the wall. "How did he do it?"

"I don't know." Sir Seth shrugged. "I guess it helps if you're dead."

Then, at that exact moment in time, King Wally walked back through the wall.

"Please forgive me. I had forgotten you're not from beyond." He smiled. "So close your eyes. That way, you'll be able to hold my hands—and while you do, you'll be able to walk right through walls, too."

"Neat-o! Let's go," Sir Ollie said excitedly, taking the king's hand.

"Me, too," Sir Seth said, closing his eyes.

The three of them walked through the wall together and stepped out into a long, luxuriously carpeted hall that stretched in both directions as far as Sir Seth and Sir Ollie could see. Pictures and paintings of regal old people adorned candlelit alcoves on both sides of the walls, all the long way down the long hallway.

"These are Poxleys, one and all," the king began to explain. But from the other side of the wall, a muffled thumping interrupted the Poxley family tour.

"Goodness gracious me, it seems we've left someone behind," he laughed heartily. "I'll go back and fetch Edith-Anne and Shasta. Wait here for me."

He disappeared back through the wall and—before you could blink—returned with two rather upset "horses."

"And now, my young friends, come with me. There's a certain Poxley I'd like you to meet."

"Oh? Who's that?" asked Sir Seth.

"Prince Quincy, of course," said the king with a scowl. "He has a lot of explaining to do."

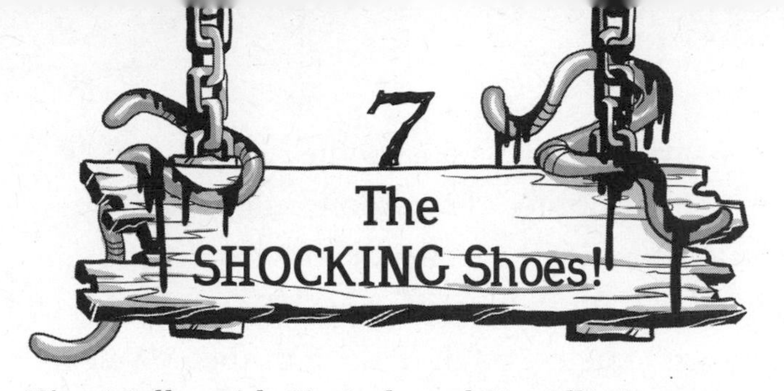

As King Wally, with Sir Seth and Sir Ollie in tow, was hurrying to the prince's room way up high on the forty-fourth floor, the first of the breathless bog runners arrived at Prince Quincy's bedroom door—and took a quick look inside. When they saw the prince admiring himself in his new soothsayer's shoes in the mirror, they immediately scurried in a blurry, toe-tangling hurry across the floor to the foot of his bed. Then, in their teeny, weeny, greedy little voices, they began babbling three different announcements at once.

"Sire! I have important news!" the first bog runner babbled in breathless Bogglegab—which is the sped-up high squeak that most bog dwellers speak.

"Sire! I have newsier news than that!" the second one excitedly interrupted the first.

"Sire! I have the newsiest news of all!" the third one excitedly interrupted all the others.

"What's this you say? You have news?" the prince roared at the three gasping bog runners. "Well, my evil little weevils, I have some news for you, too. If you ever enter my room again without knocking, I'll have the chefs prepare my favorite meal for dinner that night—bog-runner stew!"

But the three breathless busybodies were so busily babbling and gabbling, they didn't hear a word the prince said. However, he heard them.

"What's that you just said?" poxy Prince Poxley said, sitting up with interest on the side of the bed. "You say two strangely dressed fusiliers astride strange-looking steeds have just entered Poxley Castle? Why wasn't I informed of this by my spies? Where's Joyce the Voice?"

In a panic, the prince bounded from his bed and ran straight to his dresser, where he kept a large velvet bag filled with juicy bog-runner rewards. He rummaged around inside the bag, then turned with his cheeriest, most endearingest, pasted-on smile to the three greedy gremlins drooling up at him at the end of his bed.

"And now, my foul little friends, tell me, very slowly, every last bit of bog news that you know," he sneered like a snake. "And remember, whoever tells me the best news will get all the goodies I have in this bag. Now then, who wants to go first?"

No one said a word. Because if you're a bog runner, going first is the absolute worst mistake you can make. From the time a bog runner is just a bog toddler, it is taught the Rules of the Bog by its mother and father.

To be big in the bog, a bog runner must be:

1. Very nosey.
2. Very newsy.
3. Very noisy.
4. The last one to speak.

You see, if you go first, then any blabbermouths who come along after you will have news that's nosier and newsier and noisier than yours. Which means that they will get all of the prince's goodies. So that's why the three bog runners sat there without making a squeak, each waiting for one of the others to speak.

And that's what makes bog runners so greedy. But you'd probably be greedy, too, if you were a bog runner instead of being you.

The prince pulled his hand from the bag and held up a lovely, long, juicy chocolate-covered dew worm and dangled it enticingly in front of each of their excitedly twitching long noses.

"Yum, yum, yummy." He smiled his evil, weevily smile. "Who wants a nice chocolatey dew worm in their tummy?"

They all sat up on their haunches and drooled. But said nothing.

"Hurry, hurry, hurry..." Prince Quincy sneered, aware of their game. "This is the only worm I've got. So whoever goes first gets it. And the rest get to watch."

All three bog runners turned to each other and began their non-stop blithering and blabbering. All at the same time. All over again. It was hard to make any sense of what they were babbling about, but the prince's sharp ears picked out two important clues: something about two knights, and something about shoes. Uh-oh. That didn't sound good.

"What!" he gasped. "Two young knights have snuck into Poxley Castle, you say?"

Without waiting to hear one more word, Prince Quincy immediately knew what that meant. These two good knights were, no doubt, up to no good. They were probably sent all the way from Southernmost Thatchwych to steal his soothsaying shoes.

"Well, we'll see about that!" he snorted, throwing the dew worm back into the bag. He knew he would have to act now. And act fast! Yes, he must get the soothsayer's shoes safely out of sight until this annoying knightly crisis had subsided.

He reached down to take off the shoes.

But try as he might, he couldn't get Sir Shawn's shoes to budge from his feet. He tugged at one shoe, then pulled at the other.

But both shoes stayed right where they were, on both of his feet.

Desperately, he grabbed one shoe with both hands and pulled even harder, but the shoe still stayed firmly right where it was, on his left foot. Then in a final, frantic fling, the prince jumped up and down on the bed, frenziedly flailing his foot in the air until it nearly flew off with the shoe. But no matter what the prince did, Sir Shawn's shoes stayed right where they were, on both of his feet.

"Uh-oh." He squirmed in a panic. "Now what am I going to do?"

Prince Quincy nervously paced to and fro, still wearing Sir Shawn's shoes, then whirled about and paced all the way back from fro to to—trying desperately to think of what he might do. Then an idea wormed its way into his head.

"Aha! But of course, there's only one thing I *can* do!" Prince Quincy decided with a self-satisfied sneer. "If I can't take these shoes off, then I must be off—and get down to the village of Euphoria this very minute!"

Sam and Ella twittered in rat-talk and jumped up and down, nodding their heads as fast as their double chins would allow.

"I'll call a town meeting," the Prince continued, "and warn all the villagers that two unsavory Southernmost Thatchwychian thieves have come here to High Dudgeon to spread a lot of untruthful sooth about their beloved prince's new soothsaying shoes."

Oh, how Prince Quincy was warmed by the thought of marching into his kingdom's greatest town and twisting the truth so. In fact, the thought felt *so* good, he momentarily stopped thinking about everything else while he thought about it some more.

"And I wonder how goody-goody these little knights will seem to be by the time I've finished spreading all my sooth about them—and the real reason they are here."

Yes, yes, he decided. Stealing these shoes might be the best thing he'd ever done.

"Guards! Guards!" he called, as he leapt to his feet and headed to the door. "Have my horse saddled and brought round to the front door of the castle. I must get down to the village at once and announce to all the people of Euphoria and everyone, everywhere in High Dudgeon, the wonderful good news!"

The prince cackled to himself. "Indeed, good news. Now there's a *new* soothsayer wearing these shoes."

8 Bog Runners for BUDDIES?

Sir Seth scrambled to keep up with his ghostly host, who, he noticed, didn't bother to walk as they hurried down the long hall, but sort of floated instead.

"I hope I'm not going too quickly for you to keep up?" King Wally asked over one shoulder. "But we must get up to the forty-fourth floor just as fast as we can."

"It's okay. You're not going too fast at all," Sir Seth said a bit breathlessly. "But what's on the forty-fourth floor?"

"Prince Quincy's bedroom," King Wally said, but not very jollily. "He and I should have a nice little chat."

Before the king could finish, the three equally breathless bog runners burst out of one of the hall doors and ran right through King Wally's sce-through feet into Sir Seth, then into each other. Bumpity, bumpity, bump. The three very confused bog runners then slumped back onto their haunches, looked way, way up at Sir Seth, and shrieked in stark terror in their high, high squeaks as they saw Shasta bending down to give them a friendly sniff.

"It's okay. She won't hurt you," Sir Seth started to say.

But King Wally interrupted him by squeaking right back to the bog runners in Bogglegab. They were so shocked to hear a person speak in Bogglegab, they immediately forgot all about Shasta—who had, by this time, forgotten all about them, too—and continued gabbing with King Wally instead.

Following a quick conversation, the king turned to Sir Seth and Sir Ollie. "Oh dear, we're too late. They say the prince just left the castle. With Sir Shawn's shoes still on his feet."

"Uh-oh..." Sir Ollie gasped. "Which way did he go?"

Jolly King Wally turned back to the still-blabbering bog runners and repeated the question in Bogglegab.

But before the king had even finished the question, the three bog runners scrambled to be the first one to answer. Because for some bog-runner reason, being the first one to answer isn't the same as being the first one to speak.

King Wally sighed. "They said Prince Quincy has left the castle and is on his way to Euphoria to tell everyone that you have come to High Dudgeon to steal his shoes."

"*His* shoes?" Sir Seth gasped, shaking all over with shock. "We can't let him tell the villagers that. Because it just isn't true."

The king shrugged sadly. "Well, that's what he's planning to do."

Sir Ollie reached for what was left of El Gonzo. "Unless we get there first!" he declared, holding his sword high with sudden knightly resolve.

"Right, Sir Ollie. We just can't let that happen. The time for talk is over. It's time for the Mighty Knights to ride. We must get to the village before the prince."

"Indeed you must," Jolly King Wally quickly agreed. "I'd gladly help, but unfortunately, the Poxley curse doesn't allow me to go outside the castle. So it's up to you to catch Prince Quincy before he can start spreading his untruthful sooth."

Sir Ollie look worried. "But how are we gonna catch him, Sir Seth? He's had such a long head start we'll never catch him in those mucky old bogs."

Then Sir Seth had an idea. "Sire," he said, turning to King Wally, "nobody knows the bog better than those bog runners. Could you tell them we need their help?"

"Gladly, sir knight," King Wally agreed. "But the fastest way to get to Euphoria from here is the shortcut through the Evil Weevil Woods."

"Uh, what kind of woods?" Sir Ollie suddenly wanted to know.

Even King Wally shuddered at the thought. "Without doubt, Sir Ollie, it's the awfulest place in the entire kingdom. When I was still alive, I went there—just once—to see for myself just how bad a bad place can be."

"And?" Sir Seth also suddenly wanted to know.

"It was twice as bad as bad ever gets," King Wally had to admit. "You can't move an inch into those terrible tangles without something slimy grabbing your ankles.

And wherever you go, there are slithery things with slitty green eyes and long bony fingers on the tips of their wings. Then in the murky mists and shadows, you can sort of see things that look like ogres with wings and alligator ants and other things even awfuler than that. And you still haven't been caught in the candy-floss cobwebs or swallowed up by the rattlesnake grass yet."

The king paused and wiped his brow.

"However, if you hope to get to Euphoria before Prince Quincy, the Evil Weevil Woods is, by far, the shortest and fastest way to go." He looked down at the three greedy-eyed bog runners looking back up at him. "And these little fellows are the only ones anywhere in High Dudgeon who know the way—because a bog runner's about the only thing even a weevil won't eat."

"Won't eat?" Ollie said nervously. "How do weevils feel about knights?"

"That's a good question, Sir Ollie. No one knows whether weevils eat knights or not," the king reluctantly had to admit. "Because, you see, no knight who's gone in there has ever come out. Which means you'll be the first knights to find out."

"Come on, Sir Ollie. We gotta go," Sir Seth said impatiently. "While we're standing here talking, the prince is getting farther and farther away."

"Well said, sir knight!" the king agreed, patting Sir Seth on the back—which isn't easy to do if you're a ghost. "But first, follow me. If you want the bog runners to help you, we must get some treats to reward our wily wee friends—or they won't help you at all."

"Treats?" Sir Ollie perked up. "What kind of treats?"

"Chocolate-covered dew worms, of course!" The king laughed. "It's the bog runners' favorite food."

"Oh, double yuck!" Sir Ollie said, close to a faint. "What's wrong with chocolate without any worms?"

"Well, I guess it's because bog runners hate the taste of dew worms as much as you do," the king explained quickly. "Covering them in chocolate is the only way to get a bog runner to eat them."

"Sure makes me glad I'm not a bog runner," Edith-Anne shuddered.

King Wally turned and resumed his racing pace down the long candlelit hall, until he got to a heavy wooden door, which he then walked clean through and right out of sight. Completely forgetting about Sir Seth and Sir Ollie.

After a lot of thumping and bumping and rummaging around, the king re-appeared, empty-handed.

"Oh dear, I could have sworn they were in there," he sighed, then turned to Sir Seth and Sir Ollie. "My noble young knights," he whispered, careful to avoid the prying, spying ears of the bog runners, "I'm afraid I don't know what we're going to do now..."

"How are we gonna get through the Evil Weevil Woods without the bog runners?" Sir Ollie gulped.

Sir Seth knew he had to think of something fast or the trio of weasely wee guides would be long gone. Quickly,

he knelt down on both knees and looked all three little bog runners straight in all six beady eyes.

"My friends, we need your help."

Friends? The very thought made them suddenly sit up.

"I'm asking you to be our guides through the Evil Weevil Woods. But I'm afraid we can't offer you any dew worms or rewards in return..."

Then, just as King Wally said, the three bog runners immediately lost interest and turned to leave.

"Wait, wait, wait. I have something better to offer instead. If you help us, then we will forever be your friends. And that's a promise."

The bog runners looked up at Sir Seth for quite a long time without uttering a squeak. In the corners of all six little eyes, six little tears appeared, then instantly dried. It was the first time in just over three thousand years that anyone, anywhere, ever asked a bog runner to be a friend.

All three bog runners instantly squeaked their rapid agreement in bubbling, blubbering Bogglegab.

"Does that mean yes?" asked Sir Seth, hoping he already knew the answer.

But he wasn't prepared for the answer he got. The first bog runner enthusiastically threw both arms in the air, which immediately turned its entire boggy being into a large letter Y. Then the second bog runner twisted itself into a large letter E, which is much easier for a bog runner than it is for you or me. And then, as you have probably guessed, the third bog runner turned itself into a large letter S.

"It's a YES!" Edith-Anne shouted in surprise.

Then they reached up toward Sir Seth and Sir Ollie and—for the first time in their lives—gave three great big, leaping, squeaking high-fives.

"And now, my newfound friends, we gotta give you some names," Sir Seth suggested, looking down into their happy faces. "Let's see now. Well, because you're all so fast on your feet, I think we should call you, um...Swish, Swoosh, and, er, Bruce! How about that?"

It was the first time a bog runner had ever been called something nice. The three bog runners were so excited they almost exploded, but before they could do that, Sir Seth raised his sword.

"All right...it's time for the Mighty Knights of Right & Honor to ride!" he said, turning to the others. "We'll follow Swish, Swoosh, and Bruce through the Evil Weevil Woods. They'll get us to the village before the prince!"

With full colors flying and banners held high, the Mighty Knights galloped down the long hallway and paused at the top of the endless sweep of forty-four floors of spiraling stairs.

"Now what are we gonna do, cuzzins?" Edith-Anne groaned. "It'll take all day to walk down all those stairs."

Then, babbling excitedly in mind-boggling Bogglegab, Swish, Swoosh, or perhaps it was Bruce, jumped up onto the highly polished railing that ran all the way down all forty-four floors and paused with a grin at the top.

"Ready, knights!" Edith-Anne announced after listening to the bog runners. "Watch this! Here's BDB-33..."

Then, with eyes the size of banana cream pies, the bog runner threw his paws in the air and slid down all forty-four floors—gloriously, uproariously, and completely out of control all the way.

Sir Seth looked excitedly at Sir Ollie and formed his hands into a booster. "By golly, Sir Ollie, I think I'm gonna like our new friends."

"Sure seems like it, Sir Seth. But, uh, what's a BDB?"

Edith-Anne was so excited she could hardly speak. "You're not gonna believe this, cuzzin! After three thousand years of running into all kids of problems in here, the bog runners worked out a plan to un-boggle every mind-boggling problem they've ever had! Then they wrote it all down—and called it the Bog De-Boggling book. It's the answer to all our problems."

"Oh, I get it," Sir Seth said, catching Edith-Anne's excitement. "Like, right now, we need a plan to get down forty-four floors fast...without killing ourselves when we

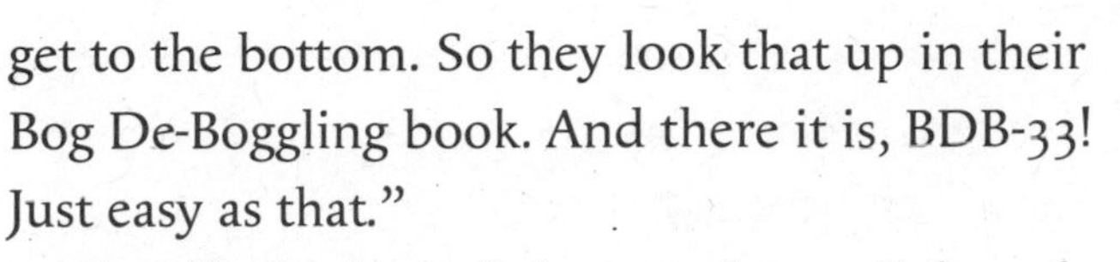

get to the bottom. So they look that up in their Bog De-Boggling book. And there it is, BDB-33! Just easy as that."

Sir Ollie looked all the way down all forty-four floors. "BDB-33? Looks like fun to me."

"Me too! So fasten your seatbelts, cuzzin." Edith-Anne grinned, climbing up on the railing. "This could be as much fun as Sloth Broth. Ready? Here we go..."

One by one, they all climbed up onto the highly polished banister that spiraled all the way down all of those stairs down to the ground floor. Then laughing and shouting at the tops of their tonsils, they slid down all forty-four floors—in a record-breaking one minute flat—and landed in a jumble of legs, arms, and armor at the feet of the two King's Kung Fu Fusiliers guarding the main castle door.

Sir Ollie was the first to look up. "Uh-oh. Looks like it's time for another quick fix."

The two large, towering guards lowered their lances, pointing them right at Edith-Anne's chest.

"Halt!" they both boomed at once.

Without being told, the bog runners immediately went to work. It could have been Swish, or maybe Swoosh, or it might even have been Bruce—it's really quite hard to say—who scurried across the great hall, jumped up onto the table, then squeeeeezed between the bars into the golden cage where Prince Quincy kept his canaries. He held up one of their bright yellow feathers.

"Ready, boggers?" he said in Bogglegab to his busy buddies. "It's time for BDB-22: Tickle time. Follow me!"

The three bog runners scooped up all the feathers they found on the floor and scurried back across the room once more. Then they ran right up the left legs of the two King's Kung Fu Fusiliers guarding the door and tickled them under their uniformed arms with the feathers.

As quick as a wink and before you could think, while the fusiliers were falling down laughing, either Swish, or Swoosh, or it might have been Bruce, jumped up and unbolted the door.

Like lightning, the Mighty Knights of Right & Honor flew out the door into the sudden, sodden gray shock of dreary old, drizzling High Dudgeon.

"Gee...I keep forgetting about the rain," Sir Ollie shuddered. "Doesn't it ever stop raining up here?"

Sir Seth smiled. "It will, Sir Ollie. It will...if we can get to the village before Prince Quincy. Just wait and see."

9 As BAD as Bad Gets

Clutching their capes in their shivering fists to keep out the unending chill, Sir Seth and Sir Ollie continued to follow quickly and quietly behind Swish, Swoosh, and Bruce—who themselves kept stopping and checking to make sure their new friends were still with them. They slowly made their way along the overgrown pathway, through the tangles and brambles and the grab of the furry burr bushes, without saying a word as they crept closer and closer to the dreaded Evil Weevil Woods.

The bog runners, who had grown up in the unending gloom of dreary High Dudgeon, scurried and scouted ahead, laughing and romping all the way—because for them, all the gloom and gray meant it was just another, typical midsummer's day.

Then Swish, Swoosh, and Bruce stopped dead in their tracks and one of them came scurrying back through the clutter of ankle-tangling vines, babbling excitedly in garbled Bogglegab.

Sir Seth looked anxiously at Edith-Anne. "What are they saying?"

"Well, they have some good news and some bad news. The good news is the gateway to the Evil Weevil Woods is just behind that tumbledown tree. But the bad news is the entrance is being guarded by a herd of elephant ants. With measles. And the bog runners don't have a BDB to get around something as enormous as that."

"Uh...elephant ants?" Sir Ollie suddenly wanted to know. "Why are they called elephant ants?"

Edith-Anne stared at him in amazement. "Well, duh. They're called elephant ants because they're ants about the size of elephants." She shrugged, as though everyone knew that. "Except, of course, elephant ants have six legs. And six feet. And measles are red speckly spots that itch like mad, no matter who's got 'em."

Sir Ollie still seemed a bit nervous. "Couldn't we, uh, sorta go around them?"

"Go around them?" Edith-Anne said with a laugh. "Cuzzin, that's a long way to walk. In fact, if you want to get around them by this time tomorrow, you should get started right about now."

Sir Ollie was about to ask another of his three thousand and three questions when—from just around the corner—came the unmistakable thundering of feet and crunching of trees that only elephant ants make when they're bashing into things with their knees.

"Did you hear that?" Sir Ollie said, with his eyes about the size of two apple pies.

They came to a clearing by the tumbledown tree and cautiously shoved aside the rubbery shubbery to take their first look at an actual, factual elephant ant with measles. And sure enough, like the bog runners said, there it was:

a for-real, for-sure elephant ant grazing by the fence! No, no. Wait. There were two. No. Wait, wait, wait. Make that three! Wait another minute. Four! No, no. There were four more than that. The whole field was full of them! There were at least ten thousand and two!

They were all wrinkled and gray, each one about the size of a house. And as all ants do, they were busily milling about, bashing and crashing and backing into each other, while dragging trees around with their trunks. Without any doubt, they were the rarest and scariest things you've ever seen.

But even scarier than that, just behind the elephant ants was a rusty iron gate with a rusty old lock—and a faded old sign beside it that said WELCOME TO THE EVIL WEEVIL WOODS. And a sign underneath it that read KEEP OUT! and TONIGHT'S MENU: KNIGHT STEW WITH FRIES. And beside that was the still-smiling skull of somebody's head! Well, maybe it was from somebody else's head. Or it could have been a zombie's instead. It's hard to tell. They all look pretty much the same in High Dudgeon half light.

"Now what are we gonna do?" Sir Seth wondered out loud.

"I remember one time my father was reading a book to me at bedtime," Sir Ollie suggested. "And it said that elephants are afraid of mice." He looked down at Swish, Swoosh, and Bruce. "What d'you think? Maybe elephant ants are afraid of mice, too."

"Sounds good to me," Sir Seth agreed, catching on to Sir Ollie's idea. "Let's hope an elephant ant thinks a bog runner's the same as a mouse."

"We can call it BDB-303," Edith-Anne said excitedly. "Okay, cuzzin, time to give it a try. Or it's gonna be a looooong walk around all those elephant ants."

She turned to Swish, Swoosh, and Bruce, and in near-perfect Bogglegab, Edith-Anne said something to the three rascally rodents that made them all giggle with glee.

"I think your father was right, cuzzin Sir Ollie. Just sit back and watch this..."

Then, for the second time that day, Swish, Swoosh, and Bruce swooped into action. They walked out into the clearing, as casually and coolly as could be, whistling and grinning. The elephant ants were so busy milling about and bashing into and bouncing off each other's backsides, they didn't notice the bog runners arrive—until it was too late.

Side by side by side and totally unnoticed, the bog runners walked right up to one of the elephant ants that had stopped to catch its breath. Swish quickly formed himself into the letter B. And then, right beside him, Swoosh formed the letter O. And so did Bruce. So together—all in a row—they spelled out a word for the elephant ant to read.

It's the same word that Swish, Swoosh, and Bruce yelled at the top of their tonsils...so loudly, in fact, that even the rain jumped back up into the air when it heard it.

It was the word BOO!!!

This started a complete stampede. The ensuing elephant-ant panic was not a pretty sight to see. One startled elephant ant shot up so fast, it jumped right out of its measles, leaving a pile of speckly red spots lying there in the grass.

All the other elephant ants immediately dropped their trees and began running in circles looking for somewhere to hide. But as you might guess, when you're as rumbling and as lumberingly large as an elephant ant, there's nowhere to hide in the middle of a field. So they all just thundered and blundered into each other and tripped over their trees, scraping most of the skin on their elbows and knees, until they tired themselves out and fell where they stood.

And while this was happening, Swish, Swoosh, and Bruce quickly turned to their new friends and frantically whistled for them to "Come on!"

"Okay, cuzzins, quick!" Edith-Anne said excitedly. "Let's go!"

No one needed to be coaxed. Everyone was up and running as fast as they could make their little legs go. They ran up to the gate and hopped over the fence, and without thinking about where they were going, they bumbled and stumbled at full speed into the Evil Weevil Woods.

Which is not a smart thing to do.

For one thing, Sir Seth, with his sword still held high, tripped over a sleeping five-hundred-pound dog-eating bog frog and flew face-first into a four-foot-deep pollywog bog. Then Sir Ollie arrived and fell over Sir Seth. Then, just as they were both getting back on their feet, Edith-Anne and

Shasta showed up and tripped over them. And when they all looked up, there was a wide-awake dog-eating bog frog glaring wide-eyed down at them—especially at Shasta.

Immediately, Sir Seth drew his sword and glared menacingly at the huge frog.

"Don't even think what you're thinking, if you're thinking what I think you're thinking," Sir Seth warned the bog frog, as he edged protectively in front of Shasta.

The frog looked at Sir Seth for a long time before answering. "That depends on what you think I'm thinking," it finally said in a soft, polite voice that startled Sir Seth.

"Well, you're probably thinking about eating my dog."

"Me? Eat your dog?" The frog smiled a thin-lipped smile. "What makes you think I want to eat your dog?"

Sir Seth shrugged. "Well, because you're called a dog-eating bog frog—"

"Ahhhhh, now I understand your confusion," the frog interrupted. "I'm called a dog-eating frog, so you thought I ate dogs. Well, then, my young friend, consider this: as far as I know, a catfish has never caught a mouse. But still, it's called a catfish. Isn't that so?"

"Huh?" Sir Seth said, completely confused.

The frog smiled and continued, "Have you ever seen a house fly?"

"No."

"Have you ever heard an elastic band?"

"No."

"So what I'm saying is...never trust what you think is inside a word. Because it might not be there."

"Why are you talking in riddles?" Sir Seth sighed, beginning to get angry. "Do you eat dogs or not?"

"Good heavens, no. Dogs give me indigestion," the bog frog said with a grin. "Let me explain. You see, although I'm called a dog-eating bog frog, the only 'dogs' that a bog frog will eat are the dogs we find under the leaves on the dogwood trees here in the bog. They're fluffy and furry, kinda like fat, velvety gnats. Everyone in here calls them bogwood dogs, although they look much more like bugs than they do like dogs... but anyhow, that's what everyone calls them. And that's why I'm called a dog-eating bog frog. Because bog dogs are all that I eat."

Sir Seth immediately put back his sword. "Oh, now I understand. I'm sorry, sir. I just assumed that a dog is a dog."

"Unless, of course, it's a horse," the frog laughed, looking at Shasta. "Well, my knightly young friend, be warned. Do not trust the words you hear in here. Trust the words you hear in your heart."

Sir Seth had no idea what the bog frog was talking about, yet somehow, it all sort of made sense. "Thank you, sir. That sounds like very good advice."

"C'mon, cuzz, let's go. This place double-scares the creeps out of me," Edith-Anne said anxiously, then whirled around face-first into a flight of fire-breathing bog bats. They flapped in circles all around her head in a flurry of fire-breathing fur for a full five seconds or more, then disappeared mysteriously back into the mists.

"W-w-what was that?!" Sir Ollie asked, almost afraid to find out.

"Oh, just some silly old bog bats," Edith-Anne explained, looking around. "And now that they've seen us, who knows? They might be off to tell the prince that we're here. Either way, we've got to keep going."

"Come on, girl. That means you too," Sir Seth said, giving Shasta a hug. "You okay?"

Shasta just smiled and gave him a lick.

However, moving quickly through the Evil Weevil Woods was much easier said than done. For a start, you'd have to edge your way around a five-hundred-pound bullfrog. Then you were instantly up to your neck in nose-nipping nettles and tricky thickets of porcupine prickles and at least six thousand kinds of viney and spiny things that pulled at your shoes with each step—if you weren't tripping over dead trees full of flocks of piranha bees and stepping on clumps of ankle-tangling snakes and grumbling bumbleberry bushes and things. And all of it in the eternal, infernal, unending rain. And you hadn't even reached the candy-floss cobwebs yet.

And nowhere, anywhere, was there a pathway to follow. Oh, make no mistake—the Evil Weevil Woods were very well named. Of all the places Sir Seth could have been, this might, by far, have been the worst.

"Where are Swish, Swoosh, and Bruce?" Sir Seth asked,

trying to see as far as his feet. "They're the only ones who know the way through this place."

In a flash, Swish came from nowhere and excitedly ran up Sir Seth's leg and jumped onto his shoulder. Then, hoisting a hawthorn needle and holding it out like a sword, Swish pointed the way they must go.

"Okay, everybody, follow the bog runners! Let's ride..."

And with that, Sir Seth took one step into the undergrowth, but before his foot hit the ground, he tripped over something and fell head first into a thicket of thick, spiny prickles. And disappeared out of sight.

"Uh...Sir Seth?" Sir Ollie called after him. "Are you all right?"

"Wow-ow-ow-ow! Look at this-iss-iss-iss," Sir Seth's voice echoed hollowly from somewhere inside the thick prickles. "I've found a secret passageway-ay-ay-ay or something-umpthing-umpthing-umpthing."

Prince Quincy impatiently ducked under the low-hanging branch of a brambled tanglefoot tree and wondered how much longer this shortcut could possibly be. He'd never really been in a rush to visit Euphoria before. If only he was already at the gate at the far end of the Evil Weevil Woods—then he could go galloping grandly down the main road to the village. But that gate seemed to remain maddeningly forever just beyond the next tree.

And so it went, hour after weary hour.

Then for four more hours after that.

"The sun is getting low in the sky. We must be getting close to the gate by now, my adorable little dollops of lard," he mumbled morosely to Sam and Ella, all the while stroking the rolls of their necks. "This so-called shortcut is more like an unending long-cut—it's taking much too much longer than I had thought. We simply must get to the Great Hall lickety quick so I can begin announcing the new sooth about me."

The two pet rats grinned and eagerly nodded their heads, as they did, no matter what he said.

"Bah!" he snorted in utter disgust. "When will I ever learn not to ask you two anything?"

But there was nobody else he could ask, except for his

rickety old horse, Mucilage. And the prince already knew the horse's answer would be the same as the rats'—a thin silly grin and a shrug.

"Ah, it's so terribly lonely being a prince," he sighed forlornly. "The only friends I have in this whole woeful world are two dreary rats and a haybag of a horse. I desperately wish I knew what it is that people don't like about warm and wonderful little old me."

Then an odd thing happened.

In the middle of his sentence, the prince stopped. And for the first time in his entire unhappy life, a strange new thought suddenly occurred to him.

"I wonder..." he wondered out loud to himself. "If I were to begin being nicer to people, perhaps people would want to be nicer to me."

However, the mere thought of being nice to people scared Prince Quincy half to death. Because for a start, he didn't know how to be nice. He had never been nice. To anyone. Anywhere. Ever. And it was quite clearly too late at this late date to begin being nice to anyone. Not now.

The prince instantly shook off that awful thought with a shudder. "Me? Being pleasant and nice to a lot of people I don't even know? Oh, deary no. That just isn't me. In fact, I don't think I like thinking this dreary, depressing thought one little bit. I do hope it gets up and goes away soon."

Then, almost as though they had just read his mind, four chicken poxhawks came swooping down and began

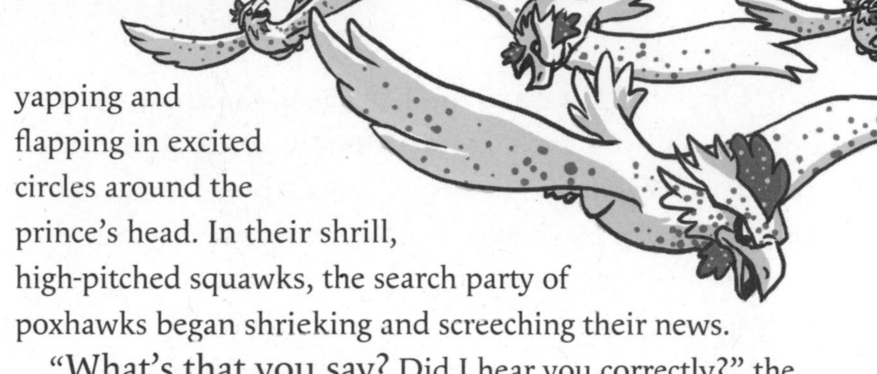

yapping and flapping in excited circles around the prince's head. In their shrill, high-pitched squawks, the search party of poxhawks began shrieking and screeching their news.

"What's that you say? Did I hear you correctly?" the prince interpreted as quickly as he could. "You say those two young Thatchwychian thieves have entered these woods? Good! That will surely slow them down. I promise you, there'll be candy-cane crickets and caramel-coated crocodile tails by the ton—for each and every one—the moment we get back to Poxley Castle."

However, the busily babbling poxhawks were still in quite a feverish flap and kept swooping in frantic circles around the prince's head.

"Aha, what's this you say? You have even more delightfully insightful new news to tell me?" he exclaimed. "I wonder what more news could there possibly be?"

As the excitedly babbling poxhawks told him their exciting new news in ear-piercing Bogglegab, Prince Quincy slapped himself on the forehead so hard he almost knocked himself off his horse.

"Oh, no! How could this be? There's an ancient secret passageway, you say, that runs from the castle all the way down to the village?" he gasped. "And, pray tell, just why is it that everyone in High Dudgeon knows of this secret passageway—except me?"

Prince Quincy was so stressed and distressed he couldn't wait for an answer. "Oh, no. This means those annoying little knights will now be able to move much quicker than me." He turned back to the poxhawks. "Quickly now, my fine feathered friends. I must be getting close to the road that leads to the village. How much farther is it from here?"

The four chicken poxhawks shreiked once again with excitement.

"Ah, good, good, good." He smiled smugly and sat up a little bit straighter. "You say it's just a short distance beyond that tanglefoot tree. Did you hear that, Mucilage?" he said, happily slapping his horse. "At last, we can fly like the wind to the village. This is your big chance to be the racehorse you've always wanted to be! You'll be worthy of a wreath of red roses—just don't expect to get one from me!"

Prince Quincy paused for a moment.

"Good heavens...did I just admit I wouldn't give her a wreath of red roses?" he muttered to himself in sudden surprise. "I just told the truth. Whatever is happening to me?"

Sir Seth sat up and brushed off billows of musty yellow dust while he looked all around at his sudden new surroundings. He simply couldn't believe his eyes. What an incredibly unexpected surprise. He was sitting in an actual, factual, for-real, touch-it, feel-it, hidden underground tunnel! It was just too cool to be true.

Maybe it was even one of those ancient secret passageways that took two bearded prisoners twenty years to dig—using only their fingernails and teeth—to escape from a bloodthirsty band of pirates holding them captive. Or something really heroic and historic like that.

The closer Sir Seth looked, the more it appeared to be an ancient underground passageway of some sort—with a bumpity cobbled brick floor underfoot and crumbly brick walls about eight feet high covered in dusty old cobwebs and must—that faded down into the darkness for as far as he could see. In fact, the place was so neat, it even echoed when he talked. Things just don't get much neater than that.

"Hey, Sir Seth-eth-eth-eth," Sir Ollie's voice echoed hollowly, as he peered down through the hole. "Are you okay-ay-ay-ay?"

"Yep. I'm fine," Sir Seth quickly assured him.

"But you're not gonna buh-lieve what I've found-ound-ound-ound. It's a secret passageway. Get down here quick-ick-ick-ick."

Sir Ollie certainly didn't have to be coaxed—because a secret passageway isn't one of those things you find every day. In fact, he was so excited, he dropped in with a heavy kerplop right on top of Sir Seth. That's when the earth around the tunnel entrance suddenly gave way. And Shasta and Edith-Anne came tumbling in, too. Followed by Swish. Then Swoosh. And finally, Bruce.

"Wow! This is too, too cool to be true," Edith-Anne exclaimed, looking eagerly down the tunnel. "If this is what I think it is, we're really in luck." She turned to Swish, Swoosh, and Bruce, who were already babbling excitedly in Bogglegab. "Well, little cuzzins, what is this thing? And where does it go?"

Swish, or Swoosh, or perhaps it was Bruce, was so excited his lips were flapping up and down at something like six hundred miles an hour.

"Well, I have some good news and some bad news," Edith-Anne said to Sir Seth and the others. "It's an ancient underground water chute, sorta like a brick sewer. It was used to shloosh water all the way down to the village and turn the creaky old waterwheel at the mill. So the good news is that the tunnel goes all the way down to the village of Euphoria. But, uh, I'm afraid there's just one little problem."

"Problem? What problem?" Sir Ollie wondered out loud.

Edith-Anne sighed sadly. "There aren't any lights."

Sir Seth's mouth fell open in shock. "No lights?"

"How are we gonna see?" Sir Ollie wanted to know.

Sir Seth peered down the dark passage. "I don't know. We need a Mighty Knightly idea, Sir Ollie...and we need it right now."

Then Swish, or Swoosh, or perhaps it was Bruce, suddenly had an idea. He scurried up Sir Seth's arm and began jumping up and down, busily jibbering and jabbering in tongue-tangling Bogglegab.

Sir Seth, of course, couldn't understand a word of it. He turned anxiously to Edith-Anne. "What's he saying?"

"Just a minute. He says he's working out a brand-new BDB."

Then, slowly, she brightened into a great big slothy

smile. "Good idea, little cuzzin. In fact, y'might even say it's brilliant!"

Without another word, the three bog runners climbed over each other back up through the opening overhead and disappeared out of sight.

"Where are they going?" Sir Ollie hopefully asked. "Do they know where the light switch is?"

"Nope. Even better than that." Edith-Anne grinned, so excited she could barely speak. "Get ready for bog runner BDB-663. They've gone to get the fire-breathing bog bats-ats-ats-ats!" These last words of Edith-Anne's echoed through the tunnel. "They'll sure brighten up things around here."

A sort of shiver ran up Sir Seth's arms, then down his back. "The fire-breathing bog bats want to help us, too? I thought all the bog bats were spies for creepy Prince Quincy," he muttered.

Edith-Anne smiled. "Well, Swoosh says the bats are just like the bog runners—they'd rather be friends with us than be tricked one more time by the prince and his pukey promises!" Her smile grew even wider. "It couldn't hurt to try."

"Those bats will brighten up and frighten up the tunnel for sure," Sir Ollie agreed.

"Not scared, are you, sir knight?" Edith-Anne teased him.

"Me? Scared of some dumb old fire-breathing bats? Not this knight, cuzzin," Sir Ollie said, although not quite convincingly. "It's just that, y'know, my mom told me bats can get tangled up in your hair, and that's bad enough. But who wants a fire-breathing bog bat getting tangled up there?"

And so, the Mighty Knights—and their horse—sat down to wait for Swish, Swoosh, and Bruce to return with the bats.

Five minutes went by.

But no Swish, Swoosh, or Bruce.

Then five more minutes went by.

Then five more.

And two more.

Then a few more after that.

Sir Seth got up and began pacing in worried circles.

That seemed like a good idea, so Sir Ollie got up and began pacing too. "Hey, Sir Seth..."

"Yeah?"

"They sure are taking a long time," Sir Ollie noticed nervously.

"Yeah, I know," Sir Seth nervously had to agree.

That wasn't quite the answer Sir Ollie wanted to hear.

"Well, y'know, while we're sitting around here doin' nothing, that pukey prince keeps getting closer and closer to the village."

"Yeah, I know," Sir Seth once again quietly agreed.

Finally, Sir Ollie stopped pacing and tried another approach. "Hey, Sir Seth..."

"Yeah?"

"D'you think maybe we made a mistake trusting a bunch of bog runners to help us?"

Sir Seth just shook his head. "It's okay, Sir Ollie. They're our friends."

"Yeah, but don't forget what Jolly King Wally said," Ollie reminded him. "A bog runner's your friend only as long as you've got something he wants. Remember? Well, what if Swish, Swoosh, and Bruce just went straight to Prince Quincy to get a better deal from him than they're gettin' from us?"

Sir Seth shook his head. "I told you. Swish, Swoosh, and Bruce are our buddies. They'll be back."

"Yeah, but how do you know?"

Sir Seth shrugged. "I don't know how I know. I just know."

That also wasn't quite the answer Sir Ollie wanted to hear. "Yeah, but we're runnin' outta time, Sir Seth. How long are we gonna wait?"

Edith-Anne interrupted with a smile. "When you run out of 'yeah, buts,' then we'll go."

Right at that exact moment—and true to their word—Swish, Swoosh, and Bruce came rushing breathlessly back down the long tunnel. They ran straight over to Edith-Anne, then looked up, grinning and nodding their heads.

And before Sir Ollie could say "yeah, but" one more time, down through the hole flew the first of the fire-breathing bog bats. Then along came four more. Then forty-four more after that. And four hundred and four more.

Followed by more and more and more and more and more bats than that.

Suddenly, the entire tunnel was all a-flit and a-flutter with swarms of rather frightening—but definitely enlightening—fire-breathing bog bats by the billions of dozens, lighting up the tunnel as though it were day. Then, one by one, the way bats always do, they flew up to the roof and hung upside down—only this time, they formed a long, long, long line of furry, fire-breathing lights that stretched down the entire length of the tunnel. It was just like the streetlights you see on your street every night.

"Hooray for our great new friends, Swish, Swoosh, and Bruce, for their brilliant new BDB!" Sir Seth shouted. "And to every one of you fire-breathing bog bats up there, you are our new friends, too—all three billion, three hundred thousand, two hundred and two of you! And now, we must ride! We have knightly deeds that need doing. And thanks to you, now we can do it!"

"Yeah!" Sir Ollie agreed, drawing his sword. "Here's to our bog-runner buddies! Now we'll be able to beat the prince—and be first to the village!"

Sir Seth, followed by his faithful steed, Shasta, started down the long dusty passageway that led to the village. Somehow, he knew in his heart they would succeed in rescuing Sir Shawn's shoes. He didn't know how he knew it. He just did.

Trust the words you hear in your heart.

The words of the bog frog had been good advice after all.

12 The Prince LEAPS Ahead!

The prince slammed the rusty old gate closed with a clang. And there, just down the cobbled brick road in the not-too-distant distance, he could see the weathered bell tower on top of the Great Hall of Euphoria peeking through the mist over the tops of the tumbledown trees.

"Well, Mucilage, you old bag of bones, the Evil Weevil Woods are behind us at last. And there, just a short gallop down the road, is the Great Hall," he said with the taste of triumph already thick in his throat. "So tally-ho! It's onward to victory we go."

As the prince swung himself back into the saddle, poor old Mucilage took one unsteady, stumbling step on the rainswept cobbled brick road, and immediately, all four of her slippy horseshoe-shod feet shot straight out in all four different directions at once. Wide-eyed with surprise, she spun completely around in a circle, then did the splits and slid backwards into the muddy ditch at the side of the road. With the prince, of course, still sitting straight up in the saddle.

"Get up, get up. This is not the time or the place to practice ballet!" Prince Quincy angrily urged her. "You've got to get up and giddy up and get going much, much faster than this. Or those soothlessly nagging knights will get to Euphoria before us."

Poor old Mucilage bumbled and stumbled her way back out of the ditch. Following four or more tumbles, she managed to get all four of her feet more or less under her. Then, somewhat unsteady—and really not ready—she started all over again, down the two miles of slippery wet bricks. In the rain.

All the while, Mucilage was spurred on by the single, unwavering thought that when she got to the village, this whole dreadful ordeal would, at last, be gloriously over. So she continued, slowly taking one unsteady step after another.

Then another.

Then one more.

And one more after that.

But with each step she took, the sky became darker and darker. Then even darker than that! It was almost as though some mysterious someone, somewhere, didn't want them to get where they were going.

Prince Quincy was beginning to panic. He could feel their head start slowly slipping away.

"No, no, no, Mucilage! This simply won't do!" Prince Quincy raged. "Get up and get galloping just like those gallant steeds in the jousting matches all do."

Then, it happened...

Have you ever gone to step down a step, then discovered that the step isn't there? Well, that's exactly what happened to Mucilage. She put out a faltering foot and felt all around on the rainy road, but the only thing there was a lot of thin air. And before she could catch her breath or her balance or anything else, Mucilage fell forward and slid, face-first, into the ditch on the other side of the road.

The prince—still sitting in the saddle, of course—at once erupted into a shouting, pouting, Prince Quincy sort of a snit. "A horse, a horse! My kingdom for a horse! Mucilage, now look what you've done. You've made me tear both knees out of my pants! How can I face my adoring public looking like some wayfaring tramp?"

He bounced up and down in the saddle.

"Get up and get going, you squeaking, creaking antique," he ranted. "We have a race to win, or haven't you heard?"

Then—with the prince still sitting straight up in the saddle, of course—Mucilage used her last ounce of strength to struggle valiantly and gallantly back to her feet. On she carried, only to once again end up skidding and skewing completely out of control. Down she tripped, down the long cobbled road, before a tall tumbledown tree finally broke her fall and—fortunately for Mucilage—not much of anything else, because the prince and his two well-cushioned rats generously absorbed most of her weight.

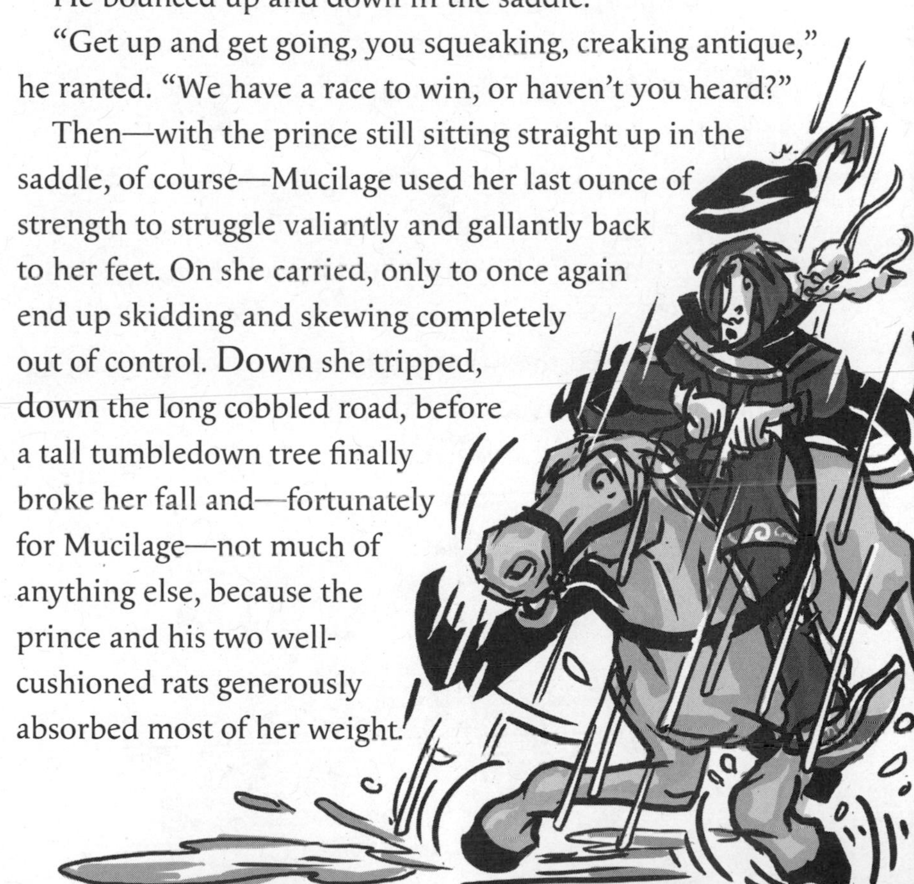

It took a full four minutes or more for Prince Quincy's world to finally slow down and stop whirling. But when, at long last, he caught his breath and took a look around, he found himself—by some impossible stroke of good fortune—sitting with his nose smunched up against a large painted sign that read "Welcome, One and All, to the Village of Euphoria."

Prince Quincy struggled to get to his knees and reached for the reins of his horse.

"Aha, Euphoria at last! I knew I could do it—because after all, I am such a perfectly competent prince, am I not!" He whooped and gloated with glee. "Step lively now, Mucilage. This is no time to sit around patting yourself on the back. Take me to the front of the Great Hall, where I can prepare for my grand entrance."

However, much to his everlasting shock and sudden surprise, when Prince Quincy turned around, he found the reins were empty. His "faithful old friend" Mucilage had finally and firmly decided that enough was enough. So she had simply seized the moment to find a new beginning somewhere else—as far from Prince Quincy as her tired old legs could carry her.

13 The FIRE-BREATHING Bog Bats

With all flags flying and pennants proudly flapping, the noble Mighty Knights of Right & Honor galloped together down the long bog bat–lit tunnel.

“How far ahead do you think Prince Quincy is?” Sir Seth asked Edith-Anne as they rode.

“Hard to say, cuzzin,” she said, gasping for breath, because galloping—as you might guess—isn’t something a sloth does very well. “Maybe a mile. Maybe two.”

“Only one mile!” Sir Ollie echoed. “How far is it to he village from here?”

Swish, or Swoosh, or perhaps it was Bruce, babbled briefly in Bogglegab to Edith-Anne.

Edith-Anne looked worried. “About three miles. Maybe more.”

Sir Ollie shot a shocked glance at Sir Seth. “Uh-oh. That means Prince Quincy has about one mile to go—and we have to go three! That doesn’t sound like a fair race to me.”

Sir Seth looked over at Edith-Anne. “We’ve got to find a way to go faster than this. Or we’ll never get to the village before the prince.”

With that, Edith-Anne stopped and held up one paw, which brought the entire procession to a tumbling, stumbling halt. "You're right," she admitted. "And it's all my fault. I'm just not a steed that's designed for speed. You'll be able to travel much faster without me. So leave me here and keep on going!"

Sir Ollie shivered all over in Mighty Knightly shock. "Leave you here? No way! Don't forget Knightly Rule Number Two: A Mighty Knight never, ever walks out on a friend, especially in the Evil Weevil Woods, where we all really need each other."

"That's right," Sir Seth agreed. "Friends stick together, no matter what."

"Well, right now, we're all together—and we need an idea," Edith-Anne groaned. "What are we gonna do?"

Then, as though it had understood every word that Sir Seth just said, one of the fire-breathing bog bats flew down and Bogglegabbed frantically in Edith-Anne's ear. She listened intently to what the bat had to say, then began excitedly jumping up and down before it could finish.

"What's he saying?" Sir Ollie anxiously asked.

"You're gonna love this, cuzzin!"

She listened carefully again to every word, then broke into a great big, happy smile. "Just like Swoosh said, the bog bats want to be our friends, too. So they've come up with a plan that'll help us get to Euphoria ahead of the prince." Edith-Anne giggled with uncontrollable glee.

"Yeah? What's the plan?" Sir Seth wanted to know.

"Bat-oil beads!"

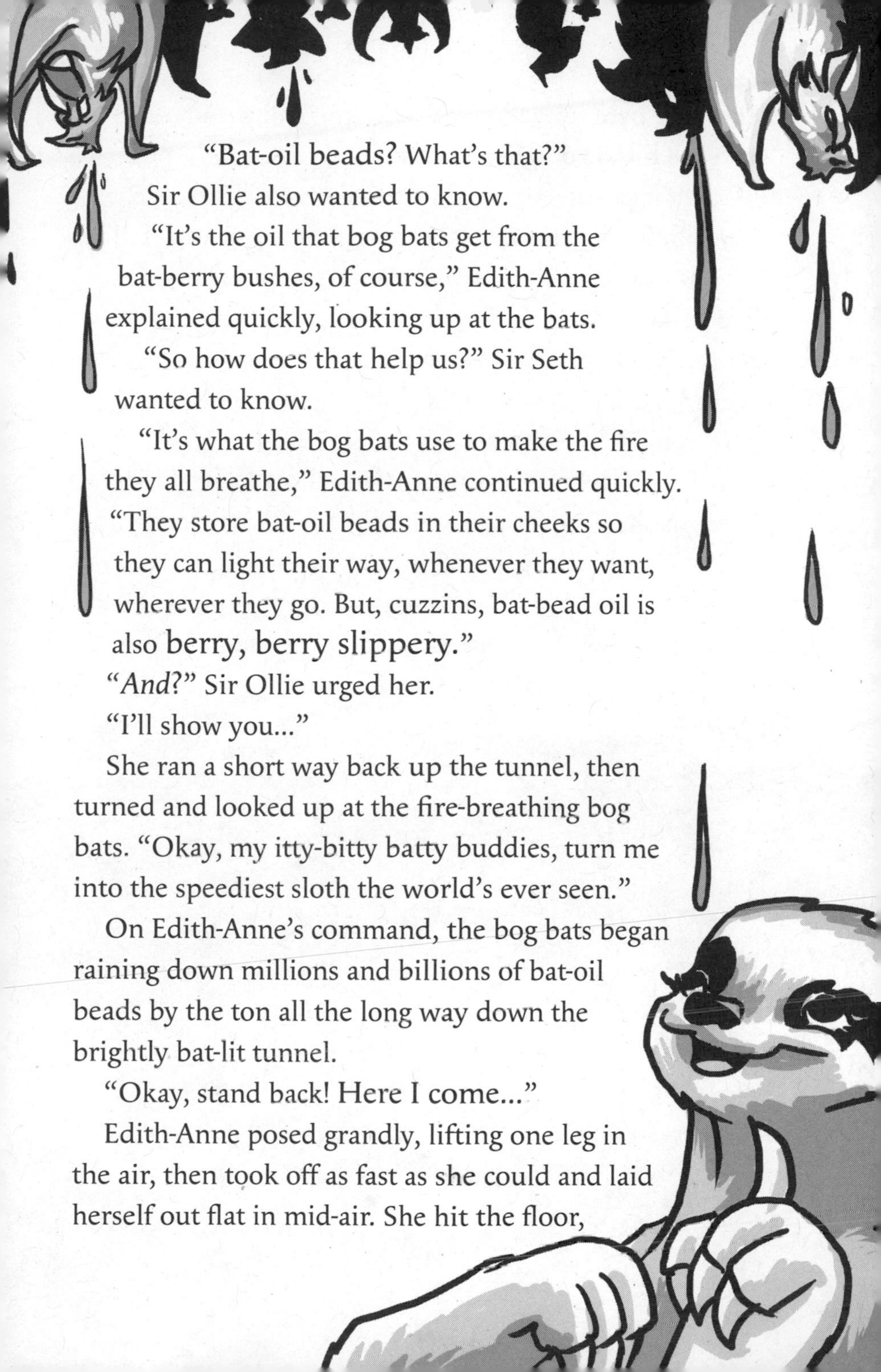

"Bat-oil beads? What's that?"

Sir Ollie also wanted to know.

"It's the oil that bog bats get from the bat-berry bushes, of course," Edith-Anne explained quickly, looking up at the bats.

"So how does that help us?" Sir Seth wanted to know.

"It's what the bog bats use to make the fire they all breathe," Edith-Anne continued quickly. "They store bat-oil beads in their cheeks so they can light their way, whenever they want, wherever they go. But, cuzzins, bat-bead oil is also berry, berry slippery."

"*And*?" Sir Ollie urged her.

"I'll show you..."

She ran a short way back up the tunnel, then turned and looked up at the fire-breathing bog bats. "Okay, my itty-bitty batty buddies, turn me into the speediest sloth the world's ever seen."

On Edith-Anne's command, the bog bats began raining down millions and billions of bat-oil beads by the ton all the long way down the brightly bat-lit tunnel.

"Okay, stand back! Here I come..."

Edith-Anne posed grandly, lifting one leg in the air, then took off as fast as she could and laid herself out flat in mid-air. She hit the floor, flat on her back, traveling at about four miles an hour. Then she hit the oily bat beads all over the floor. And it was as though someone had lit a rocket under her tail.

Whooping and hollering at the top of her tonsils, Edith-Anne flashed past Sir Seth and the rest as though they were parked. It was, by far, the fastest that Edith-Anne—or for that matter, any sloth, anywhere—ever had traveled. Or ever could. Or ever would.

"C'mon, you slowpokes and snail folks! I'm off to the village. This is even more fun than flying!" she hooted as she disappeared down the tunnel. "Fasten your seatbelts and follow me..."

"Did you see that?" Sir Ollie gasped, nudging Sir Seth in the ribs. "Now we can beat that creepy old prince to the village."

"Yep. Those bog bats just made warp speed look like slo-mo," Sir Seth excitedly agreed.

"Wait, wait. I have an idea," Sir Ollie said, looking up overhead. "I bet we can go even faster than that. C'mon, Sir Seth, help me grab one of those seed pods from the root of that tumbledown tree."

Sir Seth looked up. And immediately leapt into action. Without saying a word, he instinctively knew what Sir Ollie was thinking. "A bogsled, right?"

"Right!" Sir Ollie agreed. "We can make a bogsled out of that pod."

Sir Seth formed a booster with both hands and quickly oomphed Sir Ollie up to the top of the tunnel, just as they had done to reach the latch in the castle. "Got it?"

"Got it. Okay, comin' down!" Sir Ollie warned him, as he grabbed the long pod with both hands and jumped down. He landed with the large empty seed pod upside down on his head.

Then, working together as one, Sir Seth and Sir Ollie flipped the pod over and broke it in half, and suddenly, sitting in front of them, their homemade bogsled was waiting and ready to go.

Swish, Swoosh, and Bruce began gabbing and squeaking as fast as they could make their lips and tongues go. It was the first time someone had come up with a BDB to help them!

"Hey, you guys, you can thank us later. Right now, just hop in!" Sir Seth said, beginning to run. "Shasta!

Come on, girl. That means you, too!"

"Y'know something, Sir Seth?" Sir Ollie said as he started to run beside him.

"No. What?"

"Asking those little guys to be our friends might be the smartest thing we've ever done."

Sir Seth laughed and punched his friend on the shoulder. "For sure, Sir Ollie. You never know who your friends'll be until you give 'em the chance. Now, c'mon. Euphoria, here we come!"

And with that, the two Mighty Knights and their furry new friends took off in an oily bat-berry blur down the brightly lit tunnel.

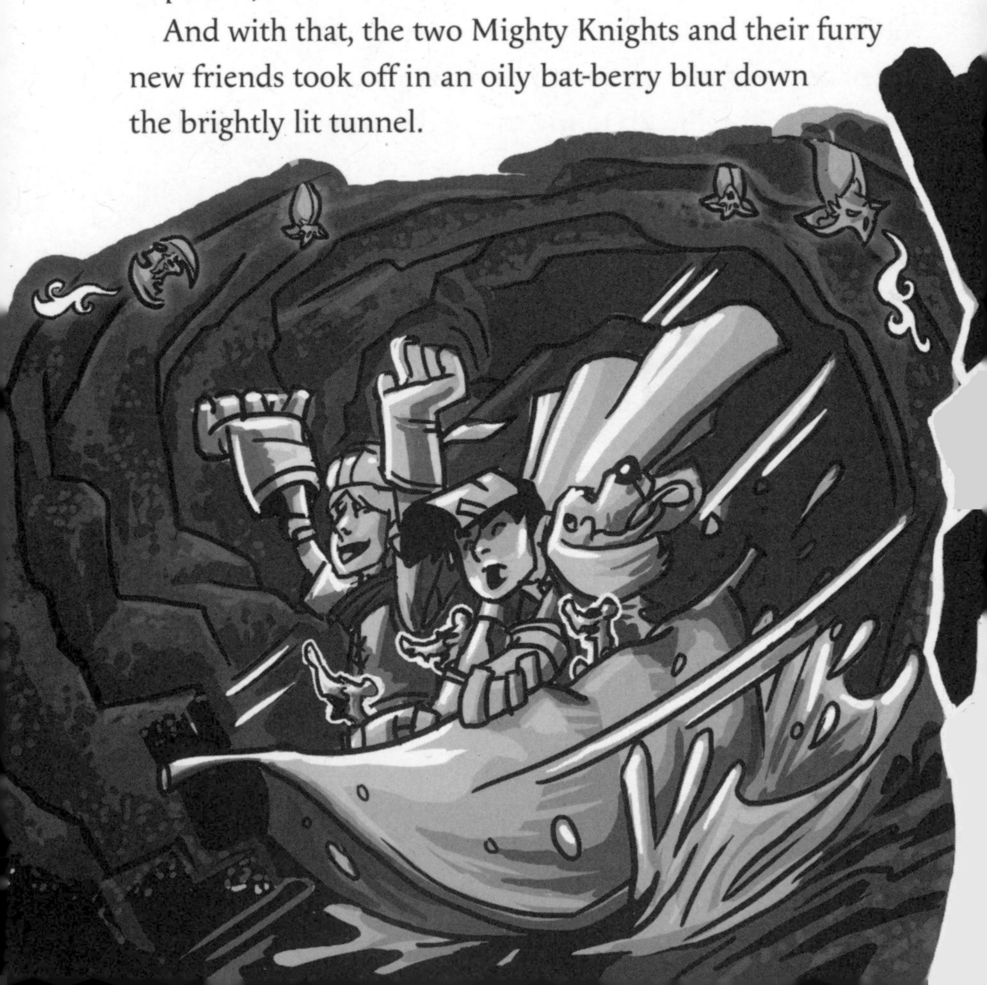

Wet, worn out, and very, very weary, Prince Quincy slowly dragged himself to his feet and tried to wipe away the unending river of rain running down his brow and into his eyes. He shuddered and shook from his chin to his shins, as the chilling rain crept all the way into the insides of his bones. Desperately, the prince struggled to keep out the cold by gathering his rain-soaked cape in a soggy bunch at his neck, while he looked all around for his magnificent bat-plumed black hat.

"Why!" he fumed in festering frustration at the unfair world closing in all around him. "Why, why, why do these terrible, unbearable things happen only to dear, adorable, huggable me?"

Then Sam, or perhaps it was Ella, squirmed out from under his bunched collar, looking for an afternoon treat.

"Not now, my bulbous little blob," the prince muttered."I have more important things to do right now than feed your overfed face."

Prince Quincy's plight was quite sad and sorry enough, but what he had no way of knowing was that when he flew face-first into the "Euphoria" sign at the town line, the letters U and P had stuck firmly to his forehead. And now, in the middle of his forehead, were the large letters, PU.

Then Ella, or perhaps it was Sam, poked its nose out from under his collar and squeaked for an afternoon treat.

"You, too?" the prince fumed. "I'm afraid, my bottomless blob, your stomach will just have to wait."

Sam and Ella looked at each other and nodded a silent agreement. Enough was enough. They decided then and there it was time to find a friendlier, more dependable neck. And before the prince could calm them or catch them, the two fat rats scrambled down his cape and scurried off into the village. Without even saying goodbye.

Prince Quincy shivered and shook with outraged indignation.

"That's all the thanks I get, is it? It's simply not fair! Not only must I walk all the way to the Great Hall—in the rain— but I must do it all alone, on my own, with no horse to carry me through the throngs of well-wishers, no courtiers or coronets to announce my arrival, no knees in my pants, no princely bat-plumed black hat on my head! Not even a fat rat for a friend," he whined out loud to no one at all. Because there was no one there to hear him.

"How very, very strange," he said to himself, performing a complete pirouette. "The village is utterly deserted, with nary a man nor a mouse, or even a flea or bee or a bird, to be seen. Where, I wonder, could everyone be? To whom should I announce my meeting?"

The prince thought about it some more. Then brightened slightly.

"Ah, but of course. Silly old me. Word has, without a

doubt, spread of my impending arrival. The entire population of dear old High Dudgeon has gloriously gathered at the Great Hall to surprise little me! Oh, dear, deary me. I must get to the main door of the Great Hall to make my grand entrance. Because as Mummy always said, it's simply not right or polite to keep everyone waiting."

Then Prince Quincy looked down at his feet. And brightened just a little bit more.

"Ah, silly me all over again...of course, of course. I'm wearing the soothsayer's magical shoes!" he sneered with sudden delight. "Soon they will help me to set the record straight. I'm so utterly weary of hearing how

everything that happens in High Dudgeon is, somehow, always my fault. It's time the true sooth about me was told. Come along, Sam and—"

As always, the prince automatically put his hand up to his shoulder to pat his two paunchy pets. But his shoulder was bare. Sam and Ella were no longer there. It felt strange and, somehow, sort of empty and sad to be so suddenly reminded that his two constant companions were gone. And beneath him, Mucilage also was no longer there.

"Ah well, they'll be back," Prince Quincy said to himself with wobbly conviction. "When they get hungry—which should be about two minutes from now—they'll come crawling back to me on their hands and their knees. Just wait and see. And once again, of course, in my usual and boundlessly benevolent way, I'll have sacks of oats and gallons of spider milk waiting to welcome them home."

The prince began trudging through the thick, sludgy mud down the main street of the village, remembering all the good times he'd had with Mucilage and Sam and Ella. And if you looked very closely, you might even have noticed a tear in one eye. Or perhaps it might have been rain.

He took a quick look back over his shoulder. "If they come home at all."

Edith-Anne sat up, groggy and google-eyed, completely surprised and gasping for breath—and tried her best to figure out what had just happened.

One minute she had been flying like lightning down the long bat-lit tunnel, then, without any warning, she found herself tumbling head over heels down a flight of stairs, ending up in a tangled-up upside-down heap on the oily tunnel floor. With her nose up against a rough wooden door.

She was still trying to gather her thoughts and straighten her nose when the bogsled carrying the rest of the knights arrived at roughly beyond warp speed. Swish, Swoosh, and Bruce landed in a heap on her lap. Whappity. Whappity. Whap. And she knew that Sir Seth and Sir Ollie and Shasta would be piling on soon after that. Which they did—plop, plop, plop—still laughing and hollering.

"Sorry," Swish, or Swoosh, or perhaps it was Bruce, said in Bogglegab to Edith-Anne, somewhat embarrassed, trying to brush her off with the end of his tail. "As you can see, we had no problem going berry, berry fast, but those bats haven't worked out a plan for stopping."

Then the bog runners looked up in shock and

immediately swarmed all over Sir Seth and Sir Ollie, excitedly breaking the latest Bogglegab news.

"I've got great news!" Swoosh babbled first, which, as you know, is something a bog runner never should do.

"No, no, no. My news is better than that!" Bruce bogglegabbed next.

"My news is the best news of all!" Swish announced proudly, having patiently waited until last. "Look who's here!" He smiled, pointing back up the tunnel.

Immediately, they all spun around to see what Swish was pointing at—and there stood Jolly King Wally with both his hands on his hips and a happy, welcoming smile on his lips.

"Aha!" he laughed with hearty delight at the sorrowful tangle the Mighty Knights had got themselves into. "So, my fine friends, you think you can run through a four-inch-thick door? Well, now you know only a ghost can do something like that."

Sir Seth couldn't believe his eyes. "King Wally! How did you get here? I thought you said—"

The king held up one hand. "I know, I know. I told you that the Poxley curse doesn't allow me to go outside the castle. But this ancient waterway is so very, very old, I had completely forgotten that it was here. It is part of the castle, so, technically speaking, when I'm inside the tunnel, I'm still officially inside the castle, if you know what I mean!"

Edith-Anne shrugged. "If you say so, Sire. It all sounds

like Gobblegab to me. I just know it's so good to see you. So where are we? And what do we do now?"

"Indeed!" King Wally said in his booming baritone voice. "Enough of this time-wasting talk. Here, we must get through this door. It leads straight into the Great Hall, where—at this very moment—the entire village is holding a most important meeting. Your timing couldn't be better. Prince Quincy is already here, preparing to make his grand entrance at the front door.

Jolly King Wally reached out to the two knights. "Quickly, each of you take one of my hands. We must get in there at once."

"Yes, Sire," Sir Ollie said, trying to take one of the king's hands. "But, uh, how can we hold something that's not quite there?"

"Have you forgotten so soon?" King Wally laughed. "You must all join hands and close your eyes."

Sir Seth closed his eyes and suddenly felt a large leathery hand firmly fit into his.

"Ready?" he smiled. "As long as I keep one foot inside this tunnel, I can pass you all into the hall. Here we go!"

With that, they all floated right through the four-inch-thick door—into the back of the Great Hall.

"You can open your eyes now," King Wally said. "The entire village has assembled to try to come up with a plan to make the kingdom of High Dudgeon a dry and good one again."

"Uh, how are they going to make High Dudgeon a

good place again?" Sir Ollie wanted to know.

"I really don't know," King Wally sighed sadly. "But after three thousand years, something must be done to stop this endless rain. And if Prince Quincy doesn't agree to the villagers' plan—and let's assume that he won't—it could mean the peace-loving people of Euphoria will have to start a revolt."

"A revolt?" Sir Ollie wondered out loud. "You mean, like, a fight?"

"Yes. Something like that," the king agreed.

"Against the King's Kung Fu Fusiliers!" Sir Seth gasped at the thought.

"Gee, that doesn't sound like much of a fair fight to me," Sir Ollie growled as he drew El Gonzo his sword and held it high over his head.

Sir Seth drew his sword, too. "We are the Mighty Knights of Right & Honor! And we will do whatever it takes..."

"...to take a wrong and turn it into a right!" they finished together.

"And don't forget," King Wally reminded them one last time, "as long as Prince Quincy is wearing Sir Shawn's truth-saying, soothsaying shoes: *the truth shall dwell in all he speaks.*"

"That's what we're afraid of," replied Sir Seth.

"So it would seem, young knight," the king agreed, "but what do those words really mean?"

Sir Seth looked up at the kindly old king with a large

lump in his heart. More than anything he had ever wanted in his entire life, he wanted King Wally to be happy again. And immediately, his mind slowly began forming a plan.

"Leave it to us, Sire," Sir Seth said in a whisper. "We'll make the name Poxley a good one again."

Ratless and horseless, bat-hatless and wet, Prince Quincy paused grandly at the main door of the Great Hall with the letters PU still on his head and sniffishly raised himself up to his loftiest, most scoffingest height. Then, with practiced panache, perfected after years of posing in front of the mirror, he majestically threw back his black cape and threw open the great door at the front of the crowded hall.

He looked quickly around at all three thousand and three unsmiling faces staring wordlessly straight back at him. The busily babbling roar of a few moments before had suddenly subsided to little more than a muttering mumble.

"G-g-good day, Your Majesty," the mayor stuttered in awe from the podium at the front of the Great Hall. "I am Gloria Astoria, the mayor of Euphoria. What an honor it is to have none other than the crown prince of High Dudgeon here at our meeting today."

With his pointy weezil nose poking straight up in the air, Prince Quincy broke into his most endearingly sneering smile and waved one hand regally at the adoring throngs of admirers who had obviously gathered at the Great Hall to greet him.

What a frightfully delightful surprise to see all of my adoring subjects gathered this day to greet and fete me this way, the prince smiled to himself in breathless surprise. *But I do wonder, how could they have known I was coming today when I scarcely knew it myself?*

At once, he quickly looked around for any sign of those two meddling knights.

But they were nowhere in sight.

I have won, I have won! he enthusiastically whooped inside himself. *Those two thugs are nowhere in sight. I can't believe it. I have beaten them here to the village. And now, the entire population of High Dudgeon will hear only me!*

At once, the prince began pushing his way through the throngs of hushed subjects to the raised stage at the front of the Great Hall, where he could begin spreading all the wonderful new news all about the wonderful new him. But as he pushed his way past the people, he couldn't help noticing that not one person in the Great Hall was smiling. Or was the least bit euphoric. Or uttered one word at all.

Undeterred by it all, when he reached the raised stage at the front of the hall, Prince Quincy turned to face all the people already facing him, with his usual winning smile and a large PU on his head.

"Well...I must admit, I hadn't planned on being here today," he said truthfully. "But now that I am more or less here, what better time could there be to tell you all the absolutely tippy-tip-topping good news about me."

He paused grandly, expecting a roar of adoring applause. But not one of the three thousand and three people cheered. Or uttered one word at all.

"What's this?" he sniffed, somewhat upset. "Is there no one here interested in hearing the cheering good news that I've got?"

No one said one word.

"Very well, then. If you don't want to hear what I came here to say, might I suggest that all of you go back to your work? And I'll tell you the good news some other day."

Then, from the far end of the Great Hall, someone said something Prince Quincy couldn't quite hear.

"Speak up," he called to the anonymous voice. "Does somebody back there have something to say?"

A leathery, weathery-faced old farmer stepped forward and repeated his plea. "Sire, we thought you already knew. Because of all this endless rain, there is no work for us to do. Or food to eat either. That's why we've come here today. Our roses are all up to their noses in rain. Our crops and our shops and our sons and daughters are almost under water as well. Sire, you must do something to rid us of this unending rain so we can begin growing our crops once again."

The mayor cleared her throat and explained. "Yes, indeed, we must put an end to all this rain and make Euphoria—and all of High Dudgeon—a glorious and euphorious place to live once again."

"I see," said the prince, without seeing much at all. "Well, I must admit, it seems you do have a bit of a problem. But surely you don't believe that a prince—even a prince as incredibly accomplished and modest as me—can stop the rain from falling, do you? There are many things a prince can do, but stopping the rain is something no one can do. Not even me."

"Ah, begging your pardon, Sire, but you can stop the rain!" another voice rang out, strongly and surely, from the back of the hall. "In fact, you are the only one in all of High Dudgeon who has the power to do it."

"Me?" the prince uttered in utter surprise.

But before he could see who it was, the voice continued, "Sire, if you recall, the only reason it's raining in High Dudgeon is all due to you."

"Me?" the prince snorted. "What makes you think that?"

The voice reminded him, "Do you remember the words of the old man's curse from long, long ago?"

"Who are you?" the prince wanted to know.

But the voice carried on, "The old man's exact words were: *You will be rid of this unending rain only when the good name of Poxley can be trusted again.* Those were his very words. Do you remember them now?"

The prince began shaking in stunned silence and shock from his curly black locks to his wet, woolly white socks and the letters PU still on his head. "You dare to imply that the good name of Poxley is unworthy of trust? I challenge you to come forward and explain yourself, sir, if you can."

Sir Seth Thistlethwaite stepped out from behind the weathered old farmer, with Sir Ollie Everghettz by his right side.

The nervous prince leaned so far forward to see who they were that he almost fell over.

"And just who, sir, are you?" the prince sniffed with instant disdain.

"I am Sir Seth Thistlethwaite, Sire."

"And I, Sire, am Sir Ollie Everghettz."

"And together," Sir Seth and Sir Ollie said as one, "we are the Mighty Knights of Right & Honor! Here to help the people of High Dudgeon however we can."

"Guards! Guards!" the prince shouted at once. "Seize these two imposters and throw them in the dungeon, and do it at once!" the prince cried, jumping up and down. "Then take out the fridge and the HD TV. And throw away the key!"

"But, Sire, we can show you how to stop the rain," Sir Seth said clearly for all the three thousand and three villagers to hear. "If you will let us."

"If I let you?" the prince sighed with a self-satisfied

sneer, glowing to overflowing, knowing full well they would fail. "By all means, sir knight, please come up here and show us how to stop the rain from falling. In fact, I insist. I'm most anxious to see how it's done," he said to the throngs.

Besides, there was very little else the prince could do to stop Sir Seth and Sir Ollie, except to allow them to make fools of themselves for all the village to see.

All six thousand and six eyes were firmly fixed on the two knights in breathless anticipation.

"Uh, Sir Seth...I sure hope you know how we're gonna get out of this," Sir Ollie whispered.

Sir Seth could still hear King Wally's words in his ear: *...the truth shall dwell in all he speaks.* He was starting to feel he knew exactly what those words meant. Purposefully, Sir Seth began walking slowly through the crowd toward the prince.

"Sire, may I ask you a question?"

"Ask me anything you wish. I have nothing to hide." The prince smirked from ear to ear, believing Sir Seth was simply stalling for time. "So, yes, by all means. Be my guest."

Sir Seth kept moving toward him. "Those shoes you are wearing. Where did you get them?"

Immediately, all six thousand and six curious eyes focused on the soothsayer's red silken shoes.

"Before you answer, Sire, you realize, of course, that whoever wears those truth-saying soothsayer's shoes must tell the truth."

Prince Quincy did his best to sniff with deep disdain. "The truth?"

"Yes, Sire. There's magic in those shoes—placed there by the Truth Fairy herself—that forces the wearer to speak only the truth."

Prince Quincy stared in knee-numbing fright at the approaching young knight, trying to think of something to say. *Tell the truth? Is that what this self-satisfied little knight said? No, no. That can't be right at all!* But suddenly, he knew deep down in his heart, that as long as he was wearing the truth-saying, soothsaying shoes, the only answer he could give was the stunning and terrible truth.

"Shoes?" he stalled, oozing with red-faced remorse. "Um, heh, heh. What shoes do you mean?"

"Those shoes on your feet," Sir Seth insisted, moving slowly closer and closer.

"These silly old shoes? The ones that somehow found their way onto my feet? Yes, well, you see, it seems they sort of belong to...well, Sir Shawn Shrood, the soothsayer of Southernmost Thatchwych."

And with those words, it had finally happened. For the first time in more than three thousand years, a Poxley had just told the truth!

And three thousand and three throats all gasped together to mark the event.

Then the most amazing thing of all happened.

The gloom in the room slowly began to shimmer with an eerie yellowish light.

Sir Seth quickly continued, "Well, then, if as you say, Sire, those shoes belong to Sir Shawn Shrood, how did they manage to get on your feet?"

Prince Quincy clamped both his hands over his mouth and turned away, knowing what the answer would be. "Well, um...I'd have to say...It appears as though someone might have stolen them, I guess," he muttered between his tightly clenched fingers.

"Was that 'somebody' you?"

"Well, not me *personally*," the prince said, hoping for one flimsy, final way out.

But he was trapped like a cat up a tree.

"Yes. I admit I ordered someone to steal them for me," he at last acknowledged in a voice so teeny and weeny that only the people in the first two rows could hear what he said.

Then, from the back of the Great Hall, the leathery-faced farmer bellowed with dewy-eyed glee, "Look! Outside the window! The rain—it's stopping. I don't believe what I see!"

All three thousand and three of the villagers looked up at the huge ornate window at the far end of the hall. And just as the weathery-faced farmer had said, the sky was brightening, as though the sun was trying to shine.

Could this mean that after three thousand years, the old man's curse was beginning to end?

Sir Seth had almost reached the stage at the front of the hall. "I have just one more question for you, Sire. Why did you steal the soothsayer's shoes?"

"Why? Well, uh..." the prince whispered, desperately trying not to say it out loud. "I just wanted to know what it would be like to be liked. I was tired of being called a pukey old prince. Then, one gloriously gray and rainy day, an idea popped into my head. The soothsayer's shoes! Aha! That was the answer. If I could get my hands on Sir Shawn Shrood's truth-saying, soothsaying shoes, I could tell everyone all kinds of wonderfully endearing things about me, and they'd have to believe everything I said was the truth!"

Sir Ollie suggested, "Sire, if you want to be liked, you don't need magical shoes. All you have to do is be likable."

"By golly, Sir Ollie," the prince agreed, "you might just be right!"

Right then and there, at that exact moment in time, the sun suddenly broke through the clouds and, for the first time in three thousand years, bathed the kingdom of High Dudgeon in its gloriously warm yellow, life-giving light.

Immediately, all three thousand and three people in the Great Hall, including Edith-Anne and Shasta, whooped and hollered and let out a thunderous roar that went on for well over a year—or so some people say who were there in the hall on that wondrous day.

Thus ended High Dudgeon's curse of darkness and rain. The whole world was once

again bright. And everyone could see their shadows again.

"Sir Seth, how can I thank you?" the prince said in amazement, stepping down to the floor. "You've put an end to the old man's curse. And to thank you for this glorious gift you've given us all, from this day forward and forevermore, I hereby declare the fifth of June as Sir Seth Thistlethwaite Day!"

The throngs of still-sodden villagers went utterly nutty, jumping with joy and cheering and weeping and chasing their shadows. Then, as one, they all swooped down and lifted Sir Seth and Sir Ollie up on their shoulders. Outside, in the sunshine, choirs were suddenly singing and church bells were happily ringing. Even Edith-Anne began jumping up and down, which is something a sloth doesn't usually do. And Shasta was barking and jumping up and down the way some knights' horses do.

"Wait, wait, wait!" Sir Seth said to the people. "Don't you see? It wasn't me who stopped the rain. It was Prince Quincy! He broke the old man's curse by telling the truth—and when he did that, he made the name of Poxley a name that can be trusted again."

When the villagers heard that, they went even more utterly nuttier with glee.

"Sir Seth is quite right," a jolly deep voice thoroughly agreed.

All of the people looked all around, but nowhere was there anyone to be seen. Then, in a puff of smoke, right beside the prince, Jolly King Wally magically appeared, even jollier—and more Wallier—than he'd ever been before.

"Oh, King Wally, it's you!" Sir Seth shouted and ran to give the king a huge, happy hug, then stopped with a start the minute he squeezed the king's hand. "King Wally, you're...not a ghost anymore. I can touch you without closing my eyes. You're a person again! Just like Sir Ollie and me."

"That I am, that I am! Thanks to you, my young friend," Jolly King Wally agreed, putting his arm around Sir Seth's tiny tinny shoulder. "Because it was you, Sir Seth Thistlethwaite—and Sir Ollie—who made the name Poxley a name that can be trusted again. And thus has the old man's curse ended. And now, it is time for me to go."

"Go?" Sir Seth echoed, looking up at the king. "Where are you going?"

"Where am I going?" King Wally roared with a thunder so loud it's said it could be heard for at least six counties or so, way beyond that fence over there. "I'm going to bed! You seem to forget that I haven't had a wink of sleep for over three thousand years. And so, Sir Seth, as you can probably guess, I am tired. Very, very tired. And for this gift of eternal rest, I shall be eternally grateful to you and Sir Ollie. Perhaps more so than you ever will know. But! Before I go, there's just one more thing I must do. Quickly. Follow me."

King Wally went over to Prince Quincy, put his arm

around his shoulder, and smiled. "I believe you are my great-grandson at least a hundred times over. It's time you began living up to all the 'greats' in front of your name. It's time you began being great!"

Prince Quincy turned to Sir Seth and Sir Ollie.

"Sir knights, I do hope you can forgive me for all the problems I've caused and for all the wrongdoings, which I must now put right..."

"I'm sure you shall be forgiven, sir, all in good time," King Wally interrupted, unsheathing his sword. "But right now, there's one more thing I must do before I go. I bid you kneel down, sir, while I name and proclaim you the new king of High Dudgeon!"

Prince Quincy couldn't believe his ears. This was the most unbelievably happy day of his entire miserable life.

King Wally touched his sword to the prince's shoulders, then looked up. "Citizens—and cuzzins—of High Dudgeon, one and all, it gives me great pleasure this day to present to you the new king of High Dudgeon... King Quincy Poxley the Thirty-Third!"

With that, all the people of High Dudgeon went absolutely and unutterably nutty with glee. They exploded with excitement and laughter, and began dancing and singing in the sun-filled streets for the next ten nights and two days!

And in the middle of this long, long, and loud celebration, a magnificent horse-drawn carriage arrived at the castle door...and out stepped King Philip Fluster the Fourth, who had come all the way from Thatchwych for the coronation, accompanied by Sir Shawn Shrood and his adorable, dimpled daughter, Lady Sheri-Sue Shrood, too!

"Welcome to happy, happy High Dudgeon," King Quincy greeted Sir Shawn Shrood with a bow—and held up Sir Shawn's magical red shoes. "I believe these shoes rightfully belong to you. Can you forgive me for this awful thing I have done?"

Sir Shawn smiled warmly. "I bid you, Sire, look around you for the answer to that. The rain in High Dudgeon has ceased, has it not? The people are happy. You are happy. And now, with these shoes returned to my feet, I am happy, too. I'd say there's much, much more magic in these shoes than anyone knew. What, pray tell, is so awful about that?"

King Quincy simply blushed and bowed with gratitude.

Sir Seth clasped Sheri-Sue's hand, and they were immediately swallowed up by the growing flow of happy people flooding through the sunshiny streets.

"Oh, Sir Seth, how can we thank you for returning my father's shoes!" Sheri-Sue said happily. "And Sir Ollie, too..."

"My lady," Sir Seth said with a bow, "it was a really exciting adventure. And for that, Sir Ollie and I thank *you*!"

Sir Ollie would have thanked Sheri-Sue, too, but he was at the banquet table, busily sampling all eight kinds of butterscotch and banana cream pies and strawberry strudel smothered in bubblegum noodles and all the other scrumdilliumptuous goodies that were there.

Finally, in the middle of the tenth day, Sir Ollie turned to Sir Seth and sighed, "Y'know, I never thought I'd say it, but I don't think I can eat one more pie. I guess that must mean it's time to go home."

"Home? Do you have to go?" Edith-Anne anxiously wanted to know. "This is the most fun I've ever had."

"Me, too," Swish sighed sadly.

"Me, too," Swoosh agreed.

"Me, too," Bruce said last, the way a smart bog runner should do."

"We'll be back," Sir Seth sighed sadly. "Soon, I hope."

"Yep. Next time you need us, we'll be here." Sir Ollie smiled and gave each of them a great big hug.

Then Sir Seth and Sir Ollie—in spite of all the villagers' and bog runners' sobs and complaints—turned to head back down the long winding trail that led home.

And like all the heroes in all the books you've ever read, the two good friends rode off into the sunset. Because for the first time in more than three thousand years, there *was* a sunset in High Dudgeon that they could ride into.

The sun began touching the tops of the trees on the far side of the pond, marking the end of another summer day.

Ollie took a bite from the meatloaf sandwich Seth had handed him. "Y'know somethin'?"

Seth looked lazily over at his friend. "No. What?"

"I really miss Edith-Anne."

Seth reeled in his fishing line. "Yeah," he agreed with a sad smile. "King Wally, too. He was a double-neat guy."

"Yeah...and sliding down that tunnel with the bog runners has gotta be the most fun I've ever had!" Ollie handed Seth a spare chocolate chip cookie he just happened to find in one pocket. "D'you think we'll ever see them again?"

Seth shrugged. "I sure hope so."

"Me, too." Ollie began reeling in his line. "So what d'you want to do tomorrow?"

Seth looked across the large pond, thinking. "Well... I was thinking maybe we could build a raft."

"A raft?" Ollie exclaimed excitedly around his cookie. "Ohhh, that's cool!"

"What d'you think we should call her?"

Ollie paused. "How about...the *Mighty Voyager*?"

Seth looked over at his best friend and raised his fishing rod high. "The *Mighty Voyager*! Yeah. I like that."

Ollie lifted his rod, too. "I can't wait till tomorrow."

The water in Puddlewater Pond is getting low. Unless somebody does something, the people of Thatchwych won't have any water to drink. Can Sir Seth and Sir Ollie solve the problem and save the day?

COMING FALL 2011

SIR SETH THISTLETHWAITE

and the Kingdom of the Caves

Richard Thake

Richard began his writing career at Maclean-Hunter Publishing Company in Toronto in 1958. He later moved into the advertising business, creating award-winning advertising campaigns for many well-known corporations and became the associate creative director of one of Canada's largest advertising agencies. A father of three grown children and a grandfather of three, Richard has finally found the time to write the Sir Seth series—a thinly disguised glimpse into his own "theater of the mind" childhood adventures with his friends in the Don River Valley and the Beach areas of Toronto.

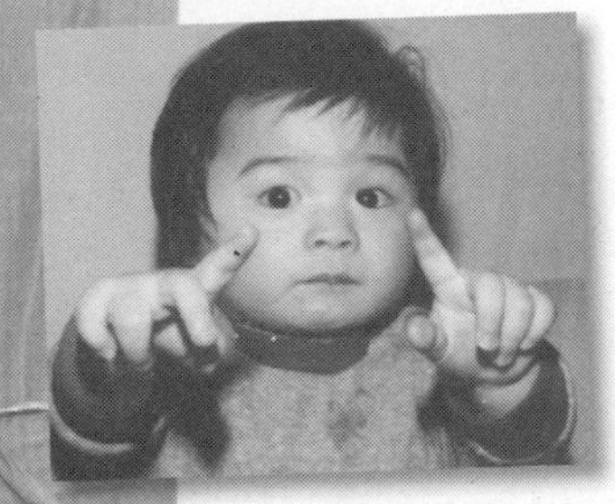

Vince Chui

Vince has spent the last six years creating illustrations and concept artwork for various entertainment properties. While at Pseudo Interactive, he worked on Xbox 360, Playstation 3, and PS2 games. Since then, he's moved on to do work with other industry staples like Sega and Paramount Pictures. He enjoys character design—when he's not out playing Ultimate Frisbee.